What did you do today?

Stories by
Anthony Varallo

2023 Winner, Katherine Anne Porter Prize in Short Fiction

University of North Texas Press
Denton, Texas

Previous Winners of the Katherine Anne Porter Prize
in Short Fiction
Polly Buckingham, series editor
Barbara Rodman, founding editor

The Stuntman's Daughter by Alice Blanchard
Rick DeMarinis, Judge

Here Comes the Roar by Dave Shaw
Marly Swick, Judge

Let's Do by Rebecca Meacham
Jonis Agee, Judge

What Are You Afraid Of? by Michael Hyde
Sharon Oard Warner, Judge

Body Language by Kelly Magee
Dan Chaon, Judge

Wonderful Girl by Aimee La Brie
Bill Roorbach, Judge

Last Known Position by James Mathews
Tom Franklin, Judge

Irish Girl by Tim Johnston
Janet Peery, Judge

A Bright Soothing Noise by Peter Brown
Josip Novakovich, Judge

Out of Time by Geoff Schmidt
Ben Marcus, Judge

Venus in the Afternoon by Tehila Lieberman
Miroslav Penkov, Judge

Printed in the United States of America.

10 9 8 7 6 5 4 3 2 1

Permissions:
University of North Texas Press
1155 Union Circle #311336
Denton, TX 76203-5017

The paper used in this book meets the minimum requirements of the American National Standard for Permanence of Paper for Printed Library Materials, z39.48.1984. Binding materials have been chosen for durability.

Library of Congress Cataloging-in-Publication Data

Names: Varallo, Anthony, 1970- author.
Title: What did you do today? / stories by Anthony Varallo.
Other titles: Katherine Anne Porter Prize in Short Fiction series ; no. 22.

Description: Denton, Texas : University of North Texas Press, [2023] |
    Series: Number 22 in the Katherine Anne Porter Prize series
Identifiers: LCCN 2023036718 (print) | LCCN 2023036719 (ebook) | ISBN
    9781574419153 (paperback) | ISBN 9781574419269 (ebook)
Subjects: LCSH: Short stories, American--21st century. | BISAC: FICTION /
    Short Stories (single author) | LCGFT: Short stories.
Classification: LCC PS3622.A725 W47 2023 (print) | LCC PS3622.A725
    (ebook) | DDC 813/.6--dc23/eng/20230807
LC record available at https://lccn.loc.gov/2023036718
LC ebook record available at https://lccn.loc.gov/2023036719

What Did You Do Today? is Number 22 in the Katherine Anne Porter Prize in Short Fiction series.

This is a work of fiction. Any resemblance to actual events or establishments or to persons living or dead is unintentional.

The electronic edition of this book was made possible by the support of the Vick Family Foundation.

For Kay McCollum, and in memory of Tom McCollum

CONTENTS

Overheard

My girlfriend and I were at a restaurant together, on the verge of breaking up again, when the man at the table next to ours leaned over and said, "Excuse me, but I couldn't help overhearing your conversation." He gave me a look that was meant to be conspiratorial or accusatory or both; I couldn't tell. "And I have to say that I agree with your girlfriend," the man said. "You really do spend too much time dwelling upon your childhood."

We hadn't been talking about me dwelling upon my childhood; we'd been discussing appetizers.

"It really is a form of self-pity," the man said, and dabbed at his lips with a white napkin. "In the final analysis."

I was about to ask him what right he thought he had to eavesdrop when our server appeared, balancing two cocktails on a tray. "Excuse me," she said, placing my girlfriend's drink on the table, "but I couldn't help overhearing what this gentleman just said to you, and I have to say I think he's right: you shouldn't leave your bath towel hanging on the shower door. That's why there's a towel rack, after all." She set my drink in front of me. "It shows just how little you think about others."

I looked at my girlfriend. I wanted her to explain to the server that I hadn't left my towel on the shower door in weeks, months even, after we'd argued about it. And I think she would have explained if the maître d' hadn't tapped me on the shoulder and said, "Excuse me, but I couldn't help overhearing your conversation, and I have to say that I agree with your server: you can't keep accusing your parents of not paying enough attention to you when you're the one who hasn't called them in months." The maître d' wore a black bow tie. His hair was slick and neat. "It's nothing more than projection."

I started to explain that, although I hadn't called my parents in a while, I texted them from time to time and occasionally sent them pictures of me and my girlfriend not quite enjoying ourselves at various events, but at that moment the busboy materialized from wherever the busboy materialized from, and said, "Excuse me—"

"Don't tell me," I said.

"But I couldn't help overhearing your conversation, and I have to say—"

"That you agree with what the maître d' just said," I said.

The busboy nodded. "You really do make everything in this relationship about *you*," he said, "to the point where the relationship isn't really even a relationship; it's more like a movie playing only inside your head." He took our silverware, although we hadn't even ordered yet. "It's a form of narcissism."

I would have refuted him if the sous chef, sommelier, line cook, parking valet, and hostess hadn't arrived, each raising a questioning finger. "Excuse me," they said. "But I couldn't help overhearing—"

My girlfriend grabbed me by the hand and led me from the table, through the crowd, and out the front door. It was chilly outside, but not too bad.

"Well," my girlfriend said.

"Well," I said.

A week later, we were engaged.

Fair Enough

Some mornings I like to open Maddy's bedroom windows and get a little air in the house. It's nice, the way the curtains move back and forth in the breeze. I sit on Maddy's bed—the one we don't use anymore since Maddy left—and watch the curtains. Just for a bit, while my husband is in the shower and can't see me on the bed. If he saw me, I know what he'd say. We don't run the air conditioner so that you can open the windows, he'd say. That's money out the window.

Fair enough, I'd say.

But this morning's breeze? Cooler than you'd imagine.

On the walls I can still see the little holes from where Maddy's posters used to hang. Pop stars, mostly, plus Harry Potter. We read the first three books together, Maddy and me, before they started getting long and dark. Before Maddy said, "Mom, you don't have to read them with me. It's *embarrassing.*"

Which was fair enough, even though I secretly finished the books later, when Maddy went off to college. Poor Dumbledore! I wanted to ask Maddy how she felt when she read that part, but I never ended up asking her, even after she dropped out and moved in with her boyfriend. I got a little sad thinking how nice it would have been for us to read that part together, so I stopped thinking about it. But I wished we had. Even after Maddy and her boyfriend stole our credit cards and disappeared to wherever.

This morning it looks like rain. The way the sky gets all green. You can smell it, that green, if you know what to smell for. I sit on the duvet we keep at the foot of Maddy's bed and watch the curtains. We've had the duvet as long as I can remember. It's the same one Maddy wrapped around her body the first time I found her in bed with her boyfriend, the two of them naked, the boyfriend a stranger, even though he smiled at me anyway, like we were old friends.

"We're not ashamed," Maddy said, "so spare us the lecture."

"Fair enough," I said, which I thought would make Maddy happy, but she only gave me this look. Like I'd failed a test where the answers were already marked in.

The wind picks up. It begins to rain. It's something, the way the raindrops get inside the window screen. The little trails they make, going this way, that way, this. I make a game of trying to guess where they're going next, but lose.

I watch them until my husband appears in the doorway. "When is this going to stop?" he asks. He races across the room and slams the windows shut. "When?"

A fair enough question, even if there is no answer.

That Night,
That Morning

That night, the parents tell the children they can stay up until nine, an hour past bedtime. It is a school night, after all, and the children must get up at six the next morning. A Tuesday night. A Wednesday morning. Just like any other school night. But this is no ordinary night, the parents know, plus the children have been begging them to stay up late. Please, the children say. Let us watch it, too. We won't be tired. We promise!

Well, the parents say.

We've stayed up late before, the children say, sensing their advantage. The children give examples. The examples consist mostly of non–school-night events, but the parents are in no mood to argue, plus the results from North Carolina are just about to be announced, so the parents do what the parents normally do when they must make a decision on the fly: they hedge. They waver. They compromise.

Listen, they tell the children. You still have to go to bed at nine, but—stop sulking, and listen to this next part, okay?—but when the results are announced, we'll wake you up and let you watch the victory speech.

All of it? the children ask.

We'll see, the parents say.

Promise you'll wake us up, the children say.

We promise, the parents say.

But at nine o'clock North Carolina still has not been called, and Florida is giving off a major whiff of disappointment. The parents dutifully march the children to bed but fail to hide their unease: they kiss the children too hastily and neglect to tickle their way out of the children's bear hugs, a nightly ritual. But the parents must hurry back to the television, back to the family room, where they've logged so many miles these past months, more televised news than they've watched since that long-ago era before children, before bedtimes, before lunchboxes, report cards, and parent-teacher meetings. They've returned to television without quite acknowledging it, somehow. If one of them turns on the late-night news, the other doesn't say anything. Instead, the two of them watch television from behind laptops and tablets, only glancing up occasionally, as if to confirm that they aren't really watching television. Who could watch this?

At ten o'clock the mother says she can't watch anymore; she's going to bed. The father says she's overreacting, even though this moment of watching her stand from the sofa and leave her tablet behind will be the moment he thinks about more than any other from that night, the moment he was suddenly alone in the family room with the television. She is being ridiculous, he thinks, without quite believing it. To counter his disbelief, the father makes a decision: when the results are announced and everything works out fine, he will wake the mother and the children and shepherd them to the television, bleary-eyed but happy, relieved. Joyful. They'll thank him for waking them, and then everyone will go to bed at last.

But the father does not go to bed at last until 1:00 a.m., and even then he cannot sleep. His mind is trying to work itself around so many things it is like; his mind reaches for a metaphor, but there's nothing there. *It is like, it is like,* his ceiling fan whispers, turning invisibly in the darkness.

That morning the father wakes the mother. What are they to tell the children? What should they say? The children will be up any minute, headed to the bathroom to perform their morning ablutions, and then they will trudge downstairs to breakfast, to backpacks, to finding their shoes from wherever it is they've left their shoes this time. They cannot let the children go downstairs alone, a break in the routine. They will have to say something after the children are done using the bathroom. The parents can hear them in there now, the sink running on full blast the way the parents have cautioned them not to. In a moment the children will open the bathroom door. They'll expect the parents to be there, ready to select their clothes for the day, ready to remind them to brush their hair.

So the parents wait outside the bathroom door, and they do not mind when the children run the sink too long, and do not wish for the sink to stop running, and do not wish for the door to open, and are still, in fact, figuring out what to say when the sink stops running and the door opens and they must tell the children the news.

Retail

The day after I got the news about my father, I drove to the mall to buy a suit. It was the middle of the afternoon, bright and hot, but the parking lot was nearly empty. Fat seagulls, with feathers the color of spent mops, congregated near the entrance doors. I had to remember where the men's store was. It had been a few years since I'd been to the mall. Who goes to the mall anymore?

When I entered the store, I saw an employee sitting behind a cash register, but it wasn't until I approached him that I realized he was sleeping. He was an older man, about my father's age, with white hair across his knuckles. A tailor's tape measure hung listlessly from his thick neck.

"Excuse me?" I said. "I need to get measured for a suit."

The man stood up suddenly and said, "You didn't like the fit?" He fumbled for the tape measure, then held it to my shoulder. "Not right?"

"No," I said. "I haven't been measured yet."

The man came from behind the register. "If I say it's the right fit, it's the right fit," he said. He instructed me to look up, wrapped the tape measure around my neck, and pulled it tight.

"That hurts," I said.

"Don't move," the man instructed. "You move it's no good." Up close, I could see hairs curling from his nostrils. The man told me my measurements.

"Those sound kind of small," I said. They were the same measurements as the last time I'd purchased a suit, back in junior high, my father taking me to the mall to get ready for graduation. But the man was already grabbing suits off the racks. He carried over a half dozen in his arms. The suits were spring colors: pastel blue, Easter white, daffodil yellow.

"Try these," he said.

"These aren't the right kind."

"You haven't even tried them!" the man said.

I tried to explain about my father, but at that moment the phone at the cash register rang, and the man scrambled to answer it. "Yes?" he said. Then, "Yes, he's here." The man gave me a look. "No, he says they aren't right." The man nodded his head at whatever the person on the other end was saying. "That's what I told him," the man said. "I said, 'But you haven't even tried yet.'" The man shook his head. "No, he wouldn't." The man held the phone out to me. "Here," the man said. "He said wants to speak to you."

"Who?" I said.

"Who do you think?"

I reached for the phone and held it to my ear. "Hello?" I said.

Before I could hear anything, a seagull landed on my arm, and then another on my shoulder, on the cash register, on the suit racks, on the man's head.

"Stupid birds!" the man shouted. "Shoo!" He swung at them with the tape measure. "How many times must I tell you?"

The Wallpaper People

When the boy turned seven, his parents wallpapered his bedroom with a colorful design they'd found on sale at the children's shop. "We thought it would brighten your room up a bit," they said.

The wallpaper was fairy-tale themed, festooned with scenes from familiar stories several years too young for the boy, but he smiled and told them he liked it. There was some pleasure, the boy was just starting to learn, in telling small lies to one's parents.

At night, though, the boy found he could not sleep. The new wallpaper gave off a whiff of glue and seemed to glow, faintly, even after the boy's parents had turned off his light. Worse, the boy found he could not stop looking at the fairy-tale scene closest to his head. It was an image from "The Elves and the Shoemaker" showing the elves sneaking into the shoemaker's shop, but the artist had drawn the elves already wearing the clothes the shoemaker's wife gives them at the end of the story, which didn't seem right. That was the whole point of the story, the boy thought. Once the elves got the clothes, the story was over. Every night the boy lay awake, staring at the elves in their incorrect clothes, his room reeking of glue. Why hadn't anyone noticed the error?

One night the boy's parents peeked their heads into the boy's room and asked him why he was still awake.

"There's something wrong with this wallpaper," the boy said.

"Wrong?" the parents said.

"Come look," the boy said. "I'll show you."

The boy showed them.

His parents smiled. They gave one another looks the boy knew meant that they thought his concerns were childish. "Well," they said, "there's just one thing to do. We have to write a letter to the wallpaper people."

The next morning his parents set the boy up at the kitchen table with a piece of paper, a pencil, and an envelope already addressed to *The Wallpaper People*, in his mother's careful script.

"What should I write?" the boy asked.

"Tell them about the mistake," his mother said, then smiled at the boy's father.

So the boy told the wallpaper people about the mistake. He told them how the elves got the clothes at the end of the story, not the beginning. How the wallpaper image didn't really make sense. The boy wrote all of this in his terrible, embarrassing handwriting. When he was finished, his parents helped him fold up the letter and seal it in the envelope. Then they watched from the front door as he walked to the mailbox and placed the letter inside.

"Don't forget to put the flag up," his parents said.

The envelope didn't even have an address on it, but the boy put the flag up anyway.

Weeks passed.

Months.

Seasons came and went.

One rainy night the boy heard someone knocking at the front door. Loud. The door rattled within the frame.

"Open up!" a voice boomed.

Through the window the boy could see lightning arcing across the sky.

"We got your letter!" the voice said.

The boy's father told the boy and the mother to stand back, then walked to the door and said, "Who's there?"

"Who's there?" the voice said, then laughed a terrifying laugh. "I said we got your letter. Who do you think it is? It's us, the Wallpaper People."

The father opened the door, which caught against the security chain.

"Oh, real nice," the voice said. "Chains the door, like we're *criminals*."

On the doorstep stood the oldest couple the boy had ever seen. A man and a woman with thin white hair and stooped posture. The man wore a rumpled hat. The woman had her face buried in the man's chest; her shoulders shook from crying.

"You see how she gets?" the man said. "You see? She takes it personally. Always has. Me, you can say whatever you want to me, I don't care." The man's voice caught. "But my wife, she's sensitive, right? She says, 'Oh, I knew I shouldn't have drawn it that way,' or, 'Oh, I knew I should have taken more time,' or, 'Oh, I knew I should have checked the story.' She gets all depressed. And I say, 'Don't worry, sweetie, you're still the best.' But she won't listen. Just stays in her room, crying." The man reached into his pocket and produced the boy's letter. "All because of goddamn letters like these!" He tore the letter in half. "Who's going to apologize to my wife? That's what I'd like to know." He threw the letter to the ground. "Who?"

And that's when the boy realized that everyone, the old woman included, had turned to face him.

The Whole World

The summer I turned thirteen, my mother invited Jerry to live with us. Jerry was a line cook at the restaurant where my mother worked who had fallen on hard times, she explained. When my mother said this, she gave me a hopeful look that was meant to imply that I should not question Jerry's presence in our home.

The day Jerry moved in, I was watching TV and eating cereal. That's what I did most of that summer: watch TV and eat cereal. Another thing I did was judge people immediately upon their looks, secretly dividing the world into Attractive or Ugly. It took me maybe half a nanosecond to place Jerry in the latter camp. Jerry was one of the ugliest people I'd ever met. His hair was stringy and wild, his cheeks pocked with acne. His glasses were preposterously large for his face, with thick bifocal lenses that caught the light in unsettling ways, as they did the moment he turned to me and said, "Is TV really *that* interesting?"

"Sometimes," I said.

"Sometimes never," Jerry said, then laughed, as if he'd said something profound. He carried in a half-dozen bags of clothes, although I never saw him wear anything besides what he wore that day: khaki shorts, closed-toe sandals, and an employee T-shirt from the restaurant where he and my mother worked, Luke's Place. TV was one of Jerry's pet peeves, I was soon to learn, along with high-fructose corn syrup, local politics, drivers who yielded right of way, period dramas, all of the Beatles' solo albums, and his stupid boss, who overvalued efficiency at quality's expense.

One day, when I was watching TV and eating cereal, Jerry asked me if I wanted to see something. Something he'd only shown to, like, two or three people in his entire life. Jerry was standing in the kitchen, wearing his employee T-shirt, his hands clasped carefully together as if cradling a baby bird. "Do you want to see?" he said.

"Sure," I said.

"Okay," Jerry said. "But you have to promise to keep it a secret."

"From my mom?"

"No," Jerry said. "She's already seen it."

"Oh," I said. "Sure thing, then."

Jerry unclasped his hands. There, on his right palm, was a ball of soap impaled with a toothpick.

"Is that a ball of soap?" I said.

Jerry smiled. He explained that this was the prototype of a sculpture he was planning to erect in Times Square, New York. I'd heard of that, right, Times Square? Anyway, the sculpture would be one hundred and twenty feet tall and eighty feet wide.

"What's it supposed to be?"

"Why, it's the whole world," Jerry said, as if this were the most obvious thing. I looked again. He had done some elaborate scrimshaw thing across the soap. The images and details were incredible—so elaborate, so precise. Suddenly, the toothpick made a kind of sensible nonsense. I drew closer. It really was the whole world.

"Just don't tell anyone," Jerry said.

These Sisters

These sisters, both teenagers, share a bedroom. The bedroom is too small for them to share, a fact that's been coming into view for the past year or so, but one that won't fully arrive until years later, when they've both moved away from the house and graduated into adulthood, when they can recall the way the bedroom felt, on those warm summer nights when they had the windows open, no breeze coming through, as an oscillating fan turned at the foot of their beds, bringing relief and then dismay in alternating intervals. Those nights, the bedroom's walls seem too close. The bedroom door, open to admit the family cat, makes faint creaking noises whose source is never understood. The family cat sleeps heavily upon one bed or the other.

Often, these sisters wake in the night. Say the cat hops off one bed or onto the other bed. Say a car passes outside, its headlights sending long parallelograms across the bedroom's walls. Say it rains. Or, more often, these sisters wake for no reason whatsoever, save the inability to turn off the movie in their heads, the one that plays happily throughout the daytime, when the movie is only too glad to let these sisters know that they are loved, cared for, admired even, to the one that plays at night, when these sisters' fears, doubts, worries, and anxieties are the sudden stars. Cruel film! The fact is, these sisters make noises at night. These sisters expel gas, without the usual discretion. These sisters toss and turn. These sisters snore. These sisters alternately blame the other, in the years that follow, for being the noisy one.

You wouldn't stop snoring! one sister claims.

What do you mean? That was you! the other says.

You were always the one who got up in the middle of the night to use the bathroom.

What? That was you! And you always left the bathroom light on.

I was the one who had to turn it off!

No, that was *me*.

The middle of the night: one sister rises from bed, touches her feet to the floor. In the other bed, the other sister snores, turns to face the wall. The beds, twin-sized, sit on opposite sides of the room to give a suggestion of space, of privacy. But it isn't enough. One sister tiptoes to the bathroom (these sisters know all the creaky spots on the floor, even in darkness) and turns the bathroom light on, discreetly, then closes the door to keep the light out. After flushing the toilet, one sister washes her hands in the too-cold water that lurches from the bathroom faucet. Her eyes are open, but not really, either. She turns the bathroom light off, opens the bathroom door. The room is quiet except for the fan, turning its head upon the beds, the cat, the other sister.

And here is the thing both sisters forget, years later, a part of the memory that slips past their recollection: the moment when, eyes not yet adjusted to the dark, one sister stands in the bathroom doorway, planning her path back to bed, and wonders, briefly, *Now, which sister am I?*

What Did You Do Today?

I woke up early and checked my phone. No texts, but three emails: CVS, Old Navy, and the Biden campaign. Apparently, Joe was concerned not to see my survey responses to his last email. Did I forget? CVS apprised me of its home delivery options. In these difficult and unprecedented times, Old Navy wanted me to know one thing and one thing only: all fleece is now 50 percent off.

I finally put those old boxes I've been meaning to put out on the curb out on the curb, then wondered if I might need those old boxes after all—who knows the next time I might be able to obtain boxes, free of fear or worry?—so I dragged those old boxes from the curb and put them back where they were before.

I checked my Instagram account. Many pictures of spectacular bread. Fabulous soups. Amazing cupcakes. I've always wanted to be one of those people who have an

Instagram account but don't actually post anything to Instagram, but I remember telling you that once and you saying, "Those are the worst kind of people."

I texted you back. You texted me back. I was watching the daily task force briefing; you were watching the daily task force briefing. We texted about the daily task force briefing for a while. I was drinking a margarita. I began to write a text where I made fun of Dr. Birx's scarves, then realized I didn't really want to start a whole text exchange where we would make fun of Dr. Birx's scarves, so I hit backspace until the text about Dr. Birx's scarves was swallowed whole.

I made a point of not checking my email for an entire morning, then went outside and halfheartedly raked leaves into an incorrect kitchen trash bag, since we're out of the tall paper ones that say things like *Yard of the Month!* or *Never Stop Improving!* on the side. It was okay for a while, but the whole time I kept imagining someone admiring me for raking leaves and not checking my email, which of course didn't happen, and which was a dumb thing to imagine in the first place. So I went inside and checked my email. Barack wanted to know if I had gotten a chance to fill out Joe's survey yet.

Yes, it was so nice to see you last night on Zoom! Right, we should do that more often. That's crazy, what your hair is doing! Sorry if I ran out of things to say after ten minutes. But you already know what I'm up to, so it's sort of hard to come up with new material. Still, good to see you. Thought I had during Zoom meeting I probably shouldn't share: at no time in human history have so many people gathered so intensely, so personally, so intimately, with so little to say to one another.

I ate Sun Chips for lunch. Plus hummus. Plus leftover Easter candy. Or wait, was that dinner? Hmm. It was 2:50 p.m. You decide!

I watched CNN and drank whiskey. Dana Bash was broadcasting from home. She was sitting in front of a bookcase. I thought I saw the Ferrante Neapolitan novels on her bookcase. I stood up from the couch to get a closer look. "What are you doing?" my wife asked, and I told her I thought I saw the Ferrante novels on Dana Bash's bookcase. "That's weird," my wife said, but I couldn't tell if she meant Dana Bash having the Ferrante novels or me spying on the TV, my face inches from the screen.

I slept in until 9:34. I texted you. I folded towels with great and unappreciated precision. I thought my hair looked kind of cool without a shower, so I skipped a shower, then felt itchy and gross the rest of the day. I answered Joe's survey. I made soup. Red lentil. I posted a photo on Instagram, if you want to see.

Uncle

Uncle says we are not to disturb him when he is in the basement. Because the basement is his place. His. Got it?

"Got it," we say, even if the basement is just our grandparents' basement. Uncle still lives with our grandparents, which is kind of funny but also not really either. We are spending the week at our grandparents' while our parents travel to the beach, to salvage their marriage, we will later learn when we are older and our parents are divorced and our grandparents and Uncle are dead, and isn't time the strangest thing?

Because now we seem to be in Uncle's car, which is crammed with bags of empty aluminum cans and translucent milk cartons. The bags are malodorous and wet. We are driving the cans and cartons somewhere, to redeem them, Uncle says, then laughs.

"You two know what that means? Redeem?" Uncle says. He takes a drag of his cigarette, exhales.

"To make up for something bad you did?" we say.

Uncle snorts. "You wish!" he says, then tosses the cigarette out the window. When Uncle laughs, we can see his yellow teeth. "It means to get money for stuff."

"Oh," we say. It's funny how the same word can mean different things, and this is also terrible and cruel and one of the many reasons that it will seem nearly impossible to ever truly know anything, we will later learn, but not now, because Uncle is taking us out for cheeseburgers and fries. After the waitress puts Uncle's plate down in front of him, Uncle takes the salt shaker and carefully, methodically, shakes row after row of salt across the entire plate, starting at the back and working toward himself, until every part of the meal has been salted.

"See what smoking does to you?" Uncle says, then takes a lusty bite of burger. "Don't start."

"We won't," we say.

"You say that now," Uncle says. "But."

"But what?"

"Stop talking to me," Uncle says.

Did we mention that Uncle talks with his mouth full? How could we when we seem to be waiting for Uncle to pick us up from swim practice—swim practice!—as we stand in the Y parking lot, dripping wet, thin towels wrapped around our waists. Poor Uncle, having to pick us up on a summer day so hot the only natural response is for Uncle to hide in his parents' basement, watching game shows while sipping Miller tallboys on the sly. Uncle tells us we aren't allowed in the car until we're 100 percent dry, then makes a show of locking the doors. We stand in the parking lot, drying off as thoroughly as we have ever dried off in our relatively short lifetimes, our bare feet burning on the pavement, while Uncle watches us, or not, from behind mirrored sunglasses. Uncle smokes menthol cigarettes. That smell! For us that smell means Uncle. Always.

Or maybe not. Maybe we will forget Uncle. Who is to say that time won't eventually erase Uncle, the way it has largely erased our grandparents, summertime, our parents' misery, and is currently working its way through the duller avenues of our childhood?

One night we sneak down into Uncle's basement. It is late. Our grandparents are sleeping. We can hear Uncle watching TV, the basement door closed, but unlocked, aha. We descend the basement stairs. We make a show of holding our fingers to our lips, as if to say, *Quiet! Don't let Uncle hear you!*

But Uncle hears us. Just as we're about to sneak up from behind and surprise him, Uncle reaches for the little cord that's connected to the only light in the basement—why are there no other lights in the basement?—and pulls it hard. The basement disappears into darkness, save for the TV, which is still bright enough that we can glimpse each other's giddy expressions.

"How many times do I have to tell you?" Uncle says.

Uncle turns the TV off. Darkness. The darkest place we have ever been. We search for each other's face, but it is no use.

"I could hear you on the stairs," we hear Uncle say, in the dark.

We begin to laugh, deep, resonant laughter that robs the air from our lungs and seems a kind of laughter we have not laughed since.

"You two make so much noise," Uncle says.

Tardy

When my high school geometry teacher, Mr. Elliot, called me on the phone and asked if I had an excuse for being tardy today, I didn't have the heart to tell him I'd graduated twenty-nine years ago. He had been a good teacher, stern but fair, whereas I'd been a lousy student, terrible at math but even worse at paying attention or getting to class on time. I could never get to class on time. I'd linger in the hallways, not exactly wanting to go to my next class but not exactly wanting to miss it either. I liked the slight thrill of showing up five minutes late, or more, the class already in full swing by the time I arrived. I'd take a seat at the back of the room, imagining that I'd been missed. *Thank God he's here now,* I imagined everyone thinking, even though I knew that was a dumb thing to imagine.

Now I listened as Mr. Elliot informed me that this tardy would be my last. After today he would have to fail me for the year. He would have no choice, he said.

I wanted to tell Mr. Elliot that I did end up failing his class, that I spent the month of June in summer school, where I continued to show up late. But what came out was, "Maybe you have the wrong person?"

"Well," Mr. Elliot said, in the voice I still remembered, the one that had so often asked me if I had a tardy slip, "I'm looking at my roll book, and it's got your name with a zero next to it."

"I'll be there as soon as I can," I said.

"Don't forget your workbook."

That was another thing I always did: forget my workbook. Where was my workbook now?

"I won't forget," I said.

"That's good," Mr. Elliot said. "We'll be expecting you soon."

But by the time I arrived at my old high school, I was already forty-five minutes late, since I had needed to stop and get gas first, and the pump I chose didn't work right, and the kid at the register said he'd have to ring up the sale separately on the other register that only his manager had the key to, and sometimes it's like, what can you do? I reached the school, parked in my old parking spot, and entered the building. Inside, the hallways were empty, just the way I remembered them, that special quality they assumed whenever I'd traveled from one end of the school to the other, late to my next class, my sneakers making tiny kissing noises on the freshly mopped tiles.

I remembered exactly where Mr. Elliot's classroom was, as easily as I remembered the proper way to turn the doorknob to call as little attention to myself as possible. I grabbed the last desk in the back row that, twenty-nine years later, still seemed to be reserved especially for me.

"Please open your workbooks to page seventy-five," Mr. Elliot said. He was standing at the front of the room, like always, where he'd scribbled some geometry problem on the chalkboard. "Who would like to solve number four?"

Mr. Elliott had aged remarkably, his sandy-brown hair swapped out for white, his smooth, well-shaven face pocked with stubble. Thick glasses in heavy black frames adorned his narrow face, giving him the unfortunate look of a bespectacled skeleton.

"Do we have a volunteer?" he asked.

I would have looked down, the way I always had whenever Mr. Elliot asked that question, but I couldn't help staring at my classmates. They, like me, had aged. The men had fared worse than the women, many of them with beer bellies and stooped shoulders, or male-pattern baldness, or heads shaved to disguise the inevitable. I tried to find the eyes of a girl I'd once sort of dated, and who, for a while, had whispered the correct answers whenever I'd shown up late to class. I found her now, but her expression was disapproving, angry even. She shook her head and mouthed something I could not hear.

"Perhaps our latest arrival would be willing to volunteer," Mr. Elliot said. He walked toward me and placed a stick of chalk on my desk. "That is," he said, "unless his willingness is also tardy today."

The class snickered. Heads turned to one another. Classmates whispered.

I stood, grabbed the chalk, and walked to the front of the room. The problem waited before me. It was one I seemed to recognize from years ago, when I'd stood in this same room at this same chalkboard. I turned the chalk over in my hand, thinking.

"Well?" Mr. Elliot said.

I'd graduated twenty-nine years ago, earned a college degree, landed a decent-enough job, earned a living wage, gotten married too young, had a kid, gotten divorced, found a new job; I'd even traveled a bit in my current position, seeing some of the world. I'd grown up, made some good choices and some bad ones, too, had taken stock of my life up to this point. I had my share of regrets and doubts, successes and setbacks.

"Well?"

I put the chalk to the board.

So much time had passed. So much experience, so much lived life, but I still didn't know the answer.

Warranty

The dryer was still under warranty, so when it shuddered to its final deafening stop—one that woke Mason's family from sleep, they let him know—Mason drove to the local appliance store to see about getting it fixed. He had to take his sons, Logan and Phillip, with him, since his wife needed time alone, she said, to do whatever it was she did when she was alone. Mason didn't mind; he was glad to get out of the house. Things always seemed a little better when he got out of the house.

Inside the store Mason dragged Logan and Phillip to the appliance service desk. A man stood behind the desk, his back to Mason. Mason was about to ask him about getting the dryer repaired when the man turned and said, "Tomorrow at ten." The man wore a blue baseball cap and gray coveralls that held a stitched-on nametag: Walt.

"I'm here about my dryer," Mason said.

"They keep you busy," Walt said, indicating Mason's sons, who had begun kicking one another. Logan grabbed Phillip by the collar. Phillip reached for Logan's arm. Mason threatened to take away their video games. Phillip cried. Logan called Phillip a crybaby.

"You're so busy, most days you don't even know how you got so busy," Walt said.

"Yeah," Mason said. Then, "I think the dryer is still under warranty, so I was hoping that—"

"Ten o'clock," Walt said. He consulted a clipboard, which held a yellow legal pad, although Mason could see that the pad was blank. "We'll see what we can do."

On the way out of the parking lot, Mason had to stop the car when Phillip threw Logan's glasses out the window. Retrieving them, it occurred to Mason that he couldn't recall telling Walt their address.

The next morning Walt arrived just as Mason's wife finished yelling at him for eating the last slices of pumpernickel; now she would have to make the children's sandwiches with hamburger buns. The hamburger buns were frozen, which would require her to thaw them in the microwave. If she thawed them in the microwave, they would get slightly chewy, and he knew how Logan and Phillip were about chewy foods, didn't he? What had happened the last time, with the baguette? Or had Mason forgotten? Mason was about to respond when he heard the front doorbell and was surprised to discover that he was elated to know that Walt had arrived.

"Ten o'clock," Mason said, opening the door. "Right on the dot."

"You had that for a while?" Walt said, indicating the crack that rose from the corner of the doorway to the roof. Mason had always meant to get that checked out at some point, but.

"I guess, maybe a year or two?" Mason said.

"Hmm," Walt said. "Well, not my parish." He asked Mason to show him the dryer.

"It's in the garage," Mason said.

"Meet you there," Walt said. Mason walked through the house to the garage and was about to open the garage door for Walt when he discovered that Walt had somehow already gotten inside the garage and was already pulling the dryer from the wall. "Has it always been like this?" Walt asked. "Right up against the wall?"

"Well," Mason said, "I guess so. Is there something wrong with that?"

"Not necessarily," Walt said, "unless." He crouched down behind the dryer and removed the hose from the back of the machine. Next, he produced a flashlight from his shirt pocket and shone the light into the hose. "Aha," he said, then gave Mason a look he wasn't sure how to read. "Let's just say it's a good thing this dryer is still under warranty." He reached into the hose, so far down that the hose swallowed his arm all the way to his elbow, and then slowly pulled it out. His fist clenched a piece of crumpled loose-leaf paper. "Looks like this is yours," Walt said, and handed the paper to Mason.

Mason unfolded the paper, not quite able to believe what he saw before him: it was a note he had written to his wife when they were first dating wherein he had tried to explain his childhood to her, in all its attendant misery, as a means of explaining who he was and what he'd thought and felt about everything up to the point of meeting her, so that she might better understand him. He hadn't seen it in years. "This?" Mason said. He felt his voice shaking. "This was in the dryer?"

Walt reached inside the dryer hose again. The hose thrashed against the machine; Walt's arm trembled in the effort. "She's putting up a fight," Walt said. The hose banged against the wall. "I'll give her that."

"Would you two keep it down in here?" Mason's wife said, materializing from the doorway. "The kids are trying to work on their solar system project." She clutched a glittering Styrofoam orb that Mason normally would have recognized as Saturn if he hadn't turned his head to Walt, who was now pulling from the hose every report card from Mason's underachieving high school career, row after row of Cs and Ds and occasional Bs and Fs.

"Honey," Mason said, "something is . . . happening here."

"Well, keep it down," his wife said.

"Yeah," Logan said, pushing though her legs. "Use your inside voice!" But his mouth was bulged with hamburger bun, so that it sounded like *ooze ore insize oyce!*

Phillip, chewing a prodigious wad of hamburger bun, too, pushed Logan aside and solemnly nodded beside him.

"The dryer," Mason said, trying to explain—but what would he explain?

"I told you to get a new one," his wife said.

Mason handed her the report cards in the same moment that Walt produced, from the hose's ribbed interior: Mason's childhood coin collection, lost since his parents had split; his one good drawing of a sailboat that his mother had framed and displayed in the downstairs bathroom for years; the mouthpiece to his old French horn, which he'd lost on the bus in fourth grade and had been made, by the band director, Mr. Perez, to search for on hands and knees; and the eulogy he'd written for Scruffy, his first and best-loved dog who'd inexplicably run away when Mason was seven, never to be seen again.

"What's all this?" his wife asked.

And Mason would have answered if Walt hadn't reached down deep into the hose, which trembled and shook and bucked from side to side and began emitting a noise so utterly strange and totally familiar that it was all Mason could do to keep from crying out.

"Well," Walt said, "here's your problem."

Scruffy scurried across the floor and licked Logan's and Phillip's fingers.

The Blanket

I don't remember much about the blanket. It was one of those handmade kinds you sometimes see in older people's homes, slung atop the back of a sofa, or folded at the foot of a bed. It was blue and gold, possibly fringed. Patterns might have played a role. Or not. Like I said, I don't remember much about it. If you were looking at a photograph of the blanket right now and asking me questions, you would probably conclude that I hardly remembered anything at all about the blanket. And you'd be a little bit right. But you'd also be a little bit wrong.

Because I remember I was nine years old when I first saw the blanket. My mother had taken me to our annual church bazaar, held in the church basement, rows and rows of tables fitted out with arts and crafts items, holiday wreaths, and poinsettias. I didn't want to go to the church bazaar. What nine-year-old wants to go to a church bazaar? I must have complained enough that my mom, in a rare moment of acquiescence, gave me a dollar and told me to look around. Maybe there was something I would like? Maybe not for me, but for someone else? Christmas was just around the corner, after all.

I wandered the bazaar for a while, the dollar in my pocket. Table after table of things I didn't want, couldn't possibly want, ever. Tea cozies and potholders. Decorative planters. Tissue box covers shaped like cats and dogs. Nativity sets fashioned from clothespins and Popsicle sticks. I stopped at each table and feigned curiosity for a while, pleased by how much interest the kindly people sitting at each table seemed to take in my presence. *Here's a nice boy with a bright future*, I imagined these people thinking, as I admired a paper towel tube pencil holder. *If only there were more young people like him!*

The blanket was spread across an entire table; I remember that. All the better to admire its needlework or stitching or embroidery or whatever. I clasped my hands behind my back as I stood before it, as if the blanket were a museum piece cordoned off with heavy ropes. The person behind the table told me about the blanket. How I could buy a raffle ticket for a chance to win it. The lucky winner would be announced at the end of the bazaar. Maybe my parents would like to buy a ticket? I nodded, then reached into my pocket and produced the dollar bill.

"One ticket, please," I said.

The person behind the table gave me a look, then handed me one half of a ticket. KEEP THIS COUPON, it read.

For the rest of the bazaar, I imagined the moment the announcer would call that number. Heads would turn.

Who had the winning ticket? And then I would clear my throat and say that I did, even though I wouldn't say it loud enough to call attention to myself. Only the people around me, whoever they happened to be, would hear. *Over here!* these people would say. *This young boy has the winning ticket!* And then I would sheepishly walk toward the announcer, head down, uncertain, clutching the winning ticket in my hand as the crowd parted in front of me, and I would feel everyone's collective thought settling around me, as warm and comforting as if they'd placed the blanket across my shoulders: *It is good and right that, of all the people who might have won this exceptional blanket, fate has chosen this young boy to be the winner.*

But I didn't win. Someone else had the winning ticket. I stood with my mother and watched as an older lady claimed my prize. People applauded and cheered. The older lady smiled. I crumpled my ticket into a tiny ball.

That was a long time ago. I can't say that I think about that blanket much, or ever, really. The blanket isn't something the means anything to me in a significant way. Except that sometimes, if I've had a long or difficult day, or something just feels wrong or a little off, and I feel that kind of discontent I now feel more often than I used to, I'll think, *Now, what is it that's got me down?* And sometimes it isn't even until later, usually when I've turned off my bedside lamp—but not my thoughts—that it will just sort of hit me.

Oh, right, I'll think, *the blanket.*

Lights

Table lamp, silver, with linen shade. Forty-watt bulb, soft white:

What his sister tells him is that she needs someone to watch the kids while she picks up Mom from the hospital. Did he really think she was going to handle this all alone? If he wants to help out for once, she says, he'll tell Jessica the situation and get on the road. Like, now. He tells his sister he'll tell Jessica, but the truth is that Jessica hasn't shared his bed for months; she sleeps in the master bedroom while he sleeps in the guest room, where they've relegated most of their least-loved furniture. Like this lamp, a leftover from Jessica's graduate school days. He observes its shade, his eyes adjusting to the light, and tells his sister he's on his way.

Ceiling fixture, kitchen, brushed nickel, four-bulb:

It's just like her brother to sleep through a night like this, the sister thinks, with Dad in the hospital and Mom at the end of her rope. That's why she's moved back home, so she can help Mom deal with everything, while her brother is off in his own little world, like usual. She sits at the kitchen table and writes a list of things he can make the kids for breakfast, in the event that she and Mom aren't back in time. Outside, it is dark. She can see herself reflected in the sliding glass doors, haloed by the kitchen light.

Car headlights, sealed beam bulbs, clear, halogen, 35 watts:

If his sister would ever listen to him, he thinks, as he drives the backroads to his parents' house, she might pick up on the fact that his marriage is falling apart. How can she not tell? But, then again, how could she, when she's so wrapped up in Dad's health problems, in Mom's fears and worries, in addition to raising two kids as a single mom? Still, to act like he's letting everyone down, when he's the one driving thirty miles in the middle of the night to watch her kids. Someone should make him a cape, he thinks, then realizes he's actually just said this aloud, to the steering wheel, to the radio, to the front windshield, where the headlights offer up the occasional deer, watching, from the shoulder of the road.

Nightlight, upstairs hallway, Snoopy themed:

She doesn't think the kids will wake this late at night, but you never know. The nightlight is from her childhood, probably an electrical hazard of some kind or another. Still, it works. That old doghouse. That familiar glow.

iPhone 8, 4.7-inch screen display, brightness: medium:

When he gets Jessica's text—*where r u?*—he can't exactly respond to it in detail. He holds the phone at steering wheel level and manages to text, *Becca called. Driving. Parents' house.* He thinks about adding more, but what else is there to say? A car, approaching in the distance, switches its high beams off.

Parking lot lights, LED, 80-watt, occasional flickering:

Hard to believe, but she still has to search for a parking place in the hospital lot, even at this time of night. Day, she should say. Early morning. Either way, she's got to hold it together for Mom, who is not terribly great at holding it together, which only upsets Dad even more, as she's reminded Mom a thousand times. She rehearses the look she will turn on Mom when Mom turns a look on her that says, *Who is it that can tell me how to be?* She is good at this look, has used it several times in the past few days, whenever Dad's health plays keep-away with them. Walking across the lot, she thinks she hears cicadas in the trees, then realizes it's the lights thrumming, clearing their radiant throats.

Porch light, three-bulb, black finish, steel frame:

She's left the key under the mat, foolishly, but it's probably okay at this time of night, he figures. The lock resists
the key at first, and he wonders why Dad hasn't gotten
around to loosening the lock with graphite, the way he
always did, and then it hits him that he's grown now, and
his marriage is over, and Dad is probably dying, and what
does the door lock matter now?

Fluorescent light, 32-watt, two-light, single cord:

Mom's look is all she needs to know. She goes to her, and
then to Dad, whose eyes are closed in the unflattering
light.

Six-inch mounted hallway light, bronze finish:

From the front hallway he can see into the kitchen, where
someone has left the overhead light on, and where he can
barely glimpse a note on the kitchen table, pinned beneath
a ballpoint pen. In his sister's scrupulous script, no doubt.
He closes the front door behind him, locks it quietly. And
that's when he hears the kids at the top of the stairs.

Lighted keypad, Trimline phone, white, wall-mounted:

Between sobs, his sister tells him the news. He says, Oh no. Says, How's Mom? Says, Oh no. Says, I will. Says, Actually, they're already up.

Ceiling fixture, kitchen, brushed nickel, four-bulb:

Why is he here? Who is on the phone? Where is their mommy? Why is he crying? To these questions he has an answer, and that answer is: he reads the note, then takes a bowl from the cabinet, grabs flour, baking powder and oil from the pantry, and milk and eggs from the fridge. He's here to make them breakfast, he tells them. What else? The kids give him sleepy, skeptical looks at first, but then he finds the chocolate chips and their faces light up.

Bad Cat

Yesterday I met the bad cat. He was lying on our neighbor's driveway, sunning himself in the last of the day's warmth. He had gray fur, slightly mottled with black, and white paws. His eyes were closed, restful. When my family and I walked past, the cat yawned and stretched his tongue the way cats sometimes do. The cat blinked at us for a moment, curiously—pleasantly, I thought.

"Here kitty-kitty!" I said. "Psst-psst!"

"*Dad*," my daughter said, "don't do that."

"Do what?" I said. "Cats love that sound."

"Please, Dad," my daughter said. "It's embarrassing."

"Plus," my son said, "I think there's something wrong with that cat."

"Don't be ridiculous," I said, and lowered my hand to the ground, as if I were cradling food, a trick from my childhood that had never failed to lure our cat, Pumpkin, out from beneath my bed. "Psst-psst! Here kitty! Hungry for a little snack?"

The cat blinked his eyes once more at me and stood. Interested.

"Dad," my daughter said, "don't trick him."

"It's not a trick," I lied.

"He thinks you have food," my son said.

"He's not going to be happy," my daughter said.

"The kids have a point," my wife said. She'd been checking out her new iPhone for the past few minutes. The walk had been her idea: we'd take a nice selfie of us walking in the neighborhood and then post it when we got home. This time of evening, the light was soft, perfect. "That cat looks a little scraggly."

"He's not scraggly," I said. I crouched to the ground and made eye contact with the cat. "Psst-psst! Here kitty!" But the moment I said it, I noticed the weeds and sticks and briars clinging to the cat's underbelly.

"Dad," my daughter said.

"Honey," my wife said. "Maybe you shouldn't."

"You guys are being ridiculous," I said. But as the cat clicked closer—one of his rear legs tapered to a wooden peg that clicked atop the asphalt—I saw that his teeth were preternaturally large and that his left ear was held together by what seemed to be industrial staples and barbed wire.

"Dad, don't," my son said.

But I wouldn't let up. I made the "psst-psst" sound even louder, and pretended to dip one hand into the other, then place something presumably yummy into my mouth. That had always worked with Pumpkin. Do that with Pumpkin, and ten seconds later he'd be purring at your feet, only too glad to have you pet him with your not-ac-tually-holding-food hand.

"Honey," my wife said. "I think that might be a bad cat."

"He's not a bad cat," I said, as the cat approached. Up close, I could see that his fur wasn't actually black and gray: the black was really a little leather jacket studded with rivets, from which something I would soon learn was a switchblade bulged. The cat was smoking a tiny ciga-rette, which sent smoke into his crusted, bloodshot eyes.

"Here kitty-kitty," I said.

"Dad," my daughter said.

When the cat nudged my hand with his nose ring, I opened my fingers to show him that there was nothing inside.

"Ta-da!" I said.

There was a moment I would like to dwell upon here, if I might. A moment when the cat looked at me with genuine surprise and perhaps even more genuine disap-pointment, before everything else unfolded. I felt in that moment, as fleeting as it was, that the cat understood something about me, about my lonely childhood, those long summer days playing umpteen bazillion games of hide-and-seek with Pumpkin, or persuading Pumpkin to watch cartoons with me on the family room sectional, or me reading all of my old Hardy Boys books to Pumpkin, who often needed me to point out the clues. It was, I would like to think, a special moment, one I know I won't soon forget.

And then the moment passed.

The first cuts of the switchblade weren't too bad; it was the nunchucks that really smarted. What with the way the bad cat struck them expertly against our ankles to get the most pain. He was good at working them with one paw while thrusting the switchblade with the other. When the bad cat bit my hand while simultaneously stabbing and nunchucking the rest of my family, I knew I should have been angry, but I couldn't help it: I felt a little proud.

Grandfather

The thing with Grandfather is, he can't help the noises he makes. Those noises are just a part of Grandfather. So we can either accept the noises Grandfather makes or we can just forget about accepting Grandfather at all. Understand? We say that we understand, but we do not understand Grandfather. We do not understand why we must be left in his care from time to time when he never seems glad to see us, never asks us anything about our lives, school, friends, interests, or hobbies, and rarely remembers our names. "You," he says, or, "Hey, Red," or, "Pipe down, Buster." Why must we listen to him snore in his armchair?

It's not that we don't like Grandfather; it's more that he doesn't seem to like us, which makes liking him feel sort of strange, like waving to someone who doesn't wave back. Why doesn't he care? We can't deny that we find his habits, rituals, and repeated phrases fascinating, though. Like, for example, the way he butters corn on the cob by dragging a fork up and down its length, the fork holding a pad of butter that melts and melts until it disappears altogether, the corn glistening in its wake. Or the way he wears a V-neck undershirt every single day, no matter the weather, no matter the time of year. We've never seen him wear anything else, really, except for when he dies, and someone hilariously puts him in a pinstriped suit—but that is later. Now we watch him eat peanuts by breaking the shell in one hand and expertly tossing the nut into his open mouth while watching Westerns. Now we hear him say, "Hits the spot." Now we watch him fall asleep like falling asleep is nothing at all. Now we hear faint, familiar bodily noises. On TV, men in Stetson hats ride white horses into the horizon.

The TV is the *idiot box*.

The refrigerator is the *ice box*.

When he dies, Grandfather says they are going to put him in *his box*.

But why does Grandfather take us to the movies, only to fall asleep in the theater? Because it is too goddamn hot to do anything else. "You could fry an egg," he says, and we do not argue, even though you can fry an egg whenever, can't you? We see movie after movie, most of them too young for us, but Grandfather says we can't beat the value: the kiddie movies are one dollar. Grandfather gets a large popcorn he doesn't share until he falls asleep and we ease the tub from his lap. Grandfather snores. Sometimes heads turn. Sometimes we get shushed.

"Sir?" an usher says. He aims a flashlight at Grandfather's feet. "No feet on the seats."

"Hey," Grandfather says, roused from dreams, "what's the big idea?"

"Sir, if you don't remove your feet, I will have to tell my manager." The usher's voice does a funny thing where it sounds like he's asking a question when he's not really asking a question.

"Keep your shirt on," Grandfather says, then puts his feet down. "Don't get all bent out of shape."

Afterward, we drive home in Grandfather's Jeep. The Jeep smells like maple syrup and motor oil. "What the hell kind of doohickey movie was that anyway?" Grandfather asks.

We tell him that's our favorite movie. We've seen it five times. Breathlessly, we recount the entire plot.

"What the hell is a wooket?" Grandfather says.

"*Wookie*," we say. But it's no use. Grandfather is already yelling at the driver in front of him, who can't hear Grandfather the way we can. Outside, cars with families in various stages of misery offer up faces impossible to read. Is life like this for everyone?

Later, we brush our teeth and get ready for bed. We know we should tell Grandfather good night, but he's already asleep in the recliner. No, we decide, we'll let him sleep. We can tell him good night some other night. Some other time.

And, much later, at Grandfather's funeral, we will recall the time he took us to see the movie about the deer whose mommy gets shot by a hunter. How the theater began to fill with sniffles and sobs. How parents and children daubed their eyes with crumpled napkins. How those sobs turned to tears, until Grandfather, waking from sleep, looked around the darkened theater and announced, "Aw, for Christ's sake, it's just a goddamn movie!" How the usher opened the exit doors to find an audience laughing at loss.

Wattage

When Davis put his mother's house up for sale, he'd felt nothing as he stripped the floral paper from the bedroom walls or liberated the upstairs hallway of its hideous wall-to-wall carpet; still, he could not bring himself to remove the lightbulb. The bulb, a 40-watt frosted General Electric, had been in the downstairs coat closet since Davis was a kid. A marvel of endurance, the bulb had survived Davis's childhood, adolescence, and adulthood, and had now outlasted his mother's illness. Open the closet door, flip the switch, and the bulb winked into life. Like it had no idea about anything.

Davis and his mother hadn't gotten along. Davis would be the first one to admit that. Still, he would say, if anyone were to accuse him of not getting along well with his mother, that she hadn't been the easiest person to get along with. Her strange habits. Her strong opinions. Her chain smoking. Her cats. Don't ask him how he got rid of the cats. She'd never approved of Davis, never liked his wives, not the first, second, nor third. Well, he'd made some mistakes too, along the way. Hadn't everyone?

The last time Davis saw his mother alive, they'd sat together in her hospice room as she drifted in and out of sleep. A pair of reading glasses kept slipping from her nose; when Davis pushed them back, his mother woke.

"You shouldn't be afraid," she said, "about what's happening to me."

"I'm not," Davis lied.

"You were always so afraid of dying. Even when you were little."

"Mom."

"You'd say, 'I don't want anyone to die, Mom! Why does everyone have to die?'"

"Mom."

"And do you remember what I told you?"

Davis didn't remember. But he didn't want to give her the pleasure of telling him what she'd said, whatever it was. No matter: she'd already fallen back asleep. Davis pushed her glasses up.

Davis had three showings last week and five scheduled for this week. The market is heating up again. Davis will sell his mother's house, despite its age. He's already had a new resident at the local medical college this close to making an offer, and a young couple relocating from out of state asking about the county's highly ranked public schools. Soon, Davis knows, he will finally be free of his mother's house.

And maybe that's why he permits himself one small pleasure whenever he gives a house tour. Davis leads the prospective buyers to the downstairs coat closet and opens the door. Invites the buyers to look inside. Do you see that lightbulb? Davis says. That lightbulb has been here since I was a kid. That same bulb! The buyers lean in, nod politely at an empty coat closet bereft of hangers. Who is this strange man who wishes to show them a lightbulb? Why does he seem on the verge of tears? The man flips the switch; the bulb glows, burns.

The Other Mothers

You'd see them sometimes, mailing a letter, or hefting a sack of groceries from the family car, or fixing your friend's lunch—the Other Mothers. All the mothers in the neighborhood who were not yours. All the mothers in those other houses, those other families, those other lives. They stood in driveways and cul-de-sacs and offered you a friendly wave when you passed by on your Schwinn three-speed, the same bike the Other Mothers had purchased for their children, who often rode alongside you, and who called these Other Mothers "Mom," and who did not think it strange that the Other Mothers required them to wear helmets, as your mother did not, something you had teased your friends about, even though you secretly wished your mother would require you to wear one, too, all the more to gain the Other Mothers' respect, approval. You'd do anything to win their admiration. Anything.

The Other Mothers were a mystery you were never quite able to solve. Why did they so often congregate on front lawns with the other Other Mothers, swapping stories and sharing laughs, their hands hidden beneath gardening gloves, their fingers clutching trowels, rakes, and sputtering hoses? What was it that was so funny? They shared some kind of Other Mother language, no doubt, known only to Other Mothers; if only you could crack its slippery code. You pedaled by, listening. The Other Mothers said things like "right" and "so true" and "mine are the same way" and "I know what you mean" and "absolutely" and "it's the same way at our house." You watched them nod to one another. Watched them make elaborate hand gestures and exaggerated facial expressions. You heard the music of their Other Mother laughter, a tune you haven't heard since.

Sometimes your friends would invite you over and then you would be in the homes of the Other Mothers. Thrilling, to see them folding laundry or watching TV or talking on the phone, a half-eaten tub of cottage cheese resting on the coffee table as the Other Mothers calmed an angry client or scheduled a meeting or handled another crisis at work, where the Other Mothers were bosses, supervisors, administrators, and branch managers, as your mother was not, something you were secretly ashamed of, although you felt guilty even thinking that. Thank God no one knew your thoughts, save for the Other Mothers, who always made a point of asking, at the exact moment you were feeling ashamed, how your mother was doing?

Fine, you'd tell them. She's great.

That's good, the Other Mothers would say. Tell her I said hello.

I will, you'd say.

But you didn't. Upon returning home, you hung your jacket on a chair, grabbed a quick snack. No one was home, or so you thought. And then you heard your mother calling your name. Was that you? How was your day? That was your mom calling you, you realized, not without happiness, love. Yours, and none other.

Hotel

The family really was excited to explore the city—they'd read so much about it!—but when they arrived at their hotel, with its striped awnings casting shade across the outdoor sushi bar, and its splendid lobby fitted out with the largest indoor fountain the children had ever seen, and its winsome concierge, Abigail, smiling from behind a serving tray upon which two perfectly chilled glasses of Chardonnay welcomingly glistened, the family decided to stay. Wasn't the hotel a part of the city too? the parents reasoned, without quite reasoning it. Didn't the children seem to love it? Hadn't they fairly begged the parents to let them fix themselves a steaming mug of hot chocolate from the complimentary café cart? Didn't they seem to cherish the lobby's overstuffed sofas, which swallowed their backsides and left their feet sticking adorably in the air? They did, the parents agreed. They did.

Their suite was even more spacious than it had looked in the online photos. How pleasant it was to open the doors to the master bedroom and the children's bedroom, so that both rooms caught the evening sun, which cast brilliant light across the shared living area, where the

children now liked to play checkers and backgammon
and Scrabble, three finds from the game cabinet beneath
the TV. The family had made a cursory glance of the TV
menu but preferred the hotel's in-house channel, which
greeted them each time they turned the TV on, and which
showed the incredible amenities available to them: a rooftop pool, a twenty-four-hour gym, a five-star steakhouse,
the outdoor sushi bar, a business center and FedEx office,
piano jazz and aperitifs each evening in the lobby, which,
it so happened, was a registered national historical land-
mark. Could anyone blame them for skipping *Stomp*?

Yes, they should make a greater effort to see the sights,
the parents agreed. Of course. Yes, they'd spent a small
fortune on tickets to the new Basquiat exhibition, the one
they'd read so many breathless reviews of; and yes, they'd
promised the children a trip to M&M's World, where they
planned to surprise them with fifty-dollar gift cards—but
that was before they'd met Abigail, who always remembered that the children's hot chocolate required extra
whipped cream and who always seemed to know the exact
moment the parents needed another pour of Chardonnay,
materializing from the lobby's impressive philodendrons
with a cloth-wrapped bottle. Who were they to say no?
What would be the point? Did they really need to have
packed the children's Sunday best, all so that the entire
family could endure the pleasant torture of *Das Rheingold*
together?

Better to spend another day at the rooftop pool, the children's favorite. There, the parents sunned themselves on chaise lounge chairs while the children splashed in the pool's tiny deep end, their arms muscled with floats. The parents heard the children's horseplay from behind iPads tipped away from the sun's glare. Drinks arrived from wherever drinks arrived from. Thick robes awaited the children, set beside towels emblazoned with the hotel's attractive logo, a gift from housekeeping, who sometimes folded the towels into seashells and seahorses. Toweled, dried, and robed, the children were allowed to press their noses against the heavy glass fencing that afforded a rooftop view of this magnificent city. The buildings! The children, daring one another to look down, made a joint discovery: atop one of the hotel's striped awnings, a white cat slept, curled into a ball.

Evenings, after happy hour Chardonnay and hot chocolate, the family ate dinner at the outdoor sushi bar or, better, the steakhouse, where everyone could order something they liked, unlike the sushi bar, where only the mother seemed to enjoy raw tuna and eel, while the rest of the family clung to tempura and California rolls, the sushi of the suburbs. The steakhouse waiters grew to know the children well and made a show of sitting down alongside them, so that they could better challenge them to a drawing contest: Who could draw the hotel? The waiters proffered their narrow pads; the children drew competing hotels. One had windows that stretched from the ground floor to the sky. Another had smiling faces where windows and doors should be. Another showed a disproportionate cat disproportionately occupying a striped awning. The waiters hung these drawings by the restaurant's antique cash register.

Oh, but everything they'd missed! Sometimes, at night, the mother would get in a mood about all the things they'd missed. The museums and galleries. The restaurants and cafés. The historical sites they'd mapped and circled in advance. The duck pond! How the children would have loved the duck pond. Would the children hold it against them? That's what the mother wanted to know: Had they made a mistake? The father consoled the mother, reminded her of all the fun they'd had since they'd arrived, all those moments of family and sharing and laughter. He gave example after example; the mother leaned her body against his and smiled. He was right, after all; they'd loved their time together in the hotel.

And that was the thought that sustained her, even as summer yielded to fall, and fall yielded to winter. Abigail brought them cabernet now, and the children used the indoor pool on the fourth floor, goodbye rooftop, and the cat no longer appeared on the awning. But the family still ate at the steakhouse, and the waiters still hung the children's drawings by the register. In fact, the family is eating there tonight. They dine at six.

The Dumb Stuff

Last night I listened to the dumb stuff. There was no one else around. No one to ask me, "Why are you listening to *that*?" No one to hold up a record in disbelief and say, "Is *this* what you're into now?" It was just me and my record player. And maybe a beer or two. Plus my floor lamp. You can't read the record jacket without the floor lamp.

I don't know how I acquired the dumb stuff. Thrift stores and yard sales mostly, I guess. Those moments when I must have looked at a record and thought, *Well, I'll probably never listen to this, but for a dollar, maybe it's sort of worth it.* Or else someone gave the dumb stuff to me. Someone who wouldn't be caught dead with this kind of stuff, but figured (correctly) that I wouldn't mind.

Even though I knew it was just the dumb stuff, I cleaned each record with the special little cloth I sometimes use, when I really care how something sounds. I held each record to the light, inspecting for scratches or potential skips. I placed the record on the turntable and timed my return to the sofa so that I would arrive just as the needle dropped, just like when I'm listening to something I actually want to hear.

The first record was pretty dumb, I'll admit it, but not terrible. There were some good things about it. The second record was better, with one or two songs I'd never noticed before, ones I knew I'd want to listen to again. I sipped one beer. And then another. The third record had one song I couldn't believe I'd never noticed before, kind of bad lyrics, sure, but that opening hook, wow, how had I never noticed that opening hook before? It felt nice to listen to the dumb stuff, with no one around to see me.

I remember when I was a kid, and I first found out about death. I was talking to an older cousin of mine, and she asked me if I knew that everybody dies, and I said people only died if they got shot by a bad guy, like in the movies, but my cousin said no, everyone dies no matter what. One day I would die, she told me. And my siblings and friends. Even my parents. Everyone.

For days after that, I had a hard time sleeping at night. I couldn't stop thinking about death. I'd stare at my alarm clock and feel this terrible sense of doom. How did anyone fall asleep at night, knowing they would one day die?

I wish I could have consoled my childhood self with what I know now. One day you'll be older and it won't seem so bad, I would say. Don't worry too much. One day you won't feel so anxious. I promise. One day you'll be free to listen to the dumb stuff.

Cruise

The world is filled with so many people we will never know; everyone on this ship, for example. See the family in matching T-shirts and sun visors, the visors topped with cat's ears? Or the same child who keeps running the length of the mezzanine at full speed, his clothes soaking wet from some source we cannot name? The pool, most likely, although the pool is crowded with children riding the backs of parents, the parents affixed to straws noisily asked to convey the last of margaritas, mojitos, and mai tais to grateful mouths. Attendants in neckerchiefs roll trash cans in from wherever and out to wherever. Walking to obtain yet another self-serve ice cream cone, we bump into eleven new strangers, our only bond our habit of saying "sorry" at the same time. Why do we want another ice cream cone?

Surely this cruise was someone's idea. Someone—us, most likely—had to pay for all of this. Which is probably how everyone else got here too. Pricey, we figure. It had to be, otherwise how would we get the opportunity to watch so many "Broadway-quality" shows with so many agreeable people we've never known? This one is top-shelf all the way, what with its seamless blend of acrobatics, rollerblading, and Sondheim tunes. We're either in awe or a little bored or maybe both; it's hard to say with our ears ringing from the applause of strangers. We'd add ours to the din, but our hands seem to be occupied by ice cream cones. When did we get those?

We tour the ship, hoping, we suppose, that we'll turn the next corner and see someone we recognize. Someone to return the world to the one we know. But the world we know seems to have been commandeered by the world of strangers, who pass us by at an alarming rate. The teenager in the neon top that proclaims MONOGAMY ROCKS! The octogenarian in a wheelchair festooned with orange flags. Not three, not four, but five adults cheerlessly dressed as Santa Claus, for reasons we'll never know. A white dog, apparently ownerless, fervently licking a fallen ice cream cone from the shuffleboard court.

We ascend stairwells teeming with passengers headed the opposite way.

"Sorry!" we say.

"Sorry!" the passengers say.

We reach the promenade deck, where so many people we do not know stand shoulder to shoulder, staring out across the flat expanse of ocean. The sun, that old standby, mysteriously hides behind thick clouds that threaten rain. Should we speak of the weather to the couple next to us, each of them taking selfies? Should we make small talk? But, wait, the clouds part. The darkness fades. The sun reemerges and permits us to see something we hadn't noticed before: another cruise ship, exactly like ours, riding the horizon. Those familiar funnels, those unmistakable masts.

"Hello! Over here!" we shout, and wave along with everyone else at what surely must be people just like us.

Interview

I didn't want the job, but I needed a job, so there I was, interviewing for the job.

"And you are?" they asked me. They were sitting at a desk. The desk was stacked high with papers, presumably resumes, presumably including mine.

I told them who I was.

"Right, right," they said, and nodded, like they had been expecting me to say that. "Of course." They shuffled through some papers, grabbed one from the top. "Aha," they said, then gave me a look I wasn't sure how to read. "Here we go." They read from the paper, all the while mumbling "yes" and "right" and "mm-hmm." After a few moments, they looked up from the paper and said, "So, could you tell us a little bit more about your decision to leave the company?"

"Well, actually I'm here to—" I began.

"No need to be shy about it," they interrupted. "Just come out and say it."

"Well, the thing is—"

"The thing is that you are unhappy here, correct?" They were looking at me from above the rims of their glasses. They offered me conspiratorial smiles. "Deeply and profoundly unhappy. Come on, don't be frightened. Speak up. You can say it now."

"Well."

"After all," they continued, "what good is an exit interview if it isn't honest? Not much, right?"

I agreed that it wouldn't do much good to lie.

"Now we're getting somewhere," they said. "Now we're really getting somewhere." They made a show of placing the paper face down on the desk, as if to indicate that we were now speaking privately, off the record. "So, let's get right to it. Can we fairly assume that this has something to do with Frank? Is that a fair assumption for us to make?"

"Well—"

"Because, let us tell you something, if we had a dime for every person who has come into this office and sat in that chair"—here, they pointed to me, to the chair I was sitting in—"and said, 'I've about had it up to here with Frank! I quit!' well, let's just say we'd have a lot of dimes." They laughed. They adjusted the papers on the desk, many of which I could now see were blank. "Or," they said, then held up a finger, "or, is it less a matter of Frank, and more a matter of workload? Because that's something else we get all the time, too. 'Sure, Frank is a total nightmare,' folks will say, 'but maybe if the workload wasn't so overbearing, I guess I could maybe deal with Frank.'"

"Hmm," I said.

"Hmm?" they said. "What does 'hmm' mean?"

"Well, I guess it means—"

"It means that you'd much prefer it if we'd stop beating around the bush with all of this Frank and workload nonsense, and just come out and ask it. Is that right?" They cleared their throats. They made dramatic neck rolls. They cracked their knuckles. "Fine. Here goes: Is this really about the vermin situation?"

"Well—"

"Because, believe us, that's not something we're just going to come out and volunteer, is it? Why would we? What would we stand to gain if the first words out of our mouth were 'vermin situation'?"

"Nothing?" I offered.

"Nothing!" they said. "That's one hundred percent the case here: nothing."

Here they made a show of shuffling through some more papers, many of which fluttered to the ground. One landed at my feet. It was the most elaborate drawing of an avocado I'd ever seen. Its skin was dappled with exotic light. The avocado glittered and shone.

"Aha!" they said, and slammed a piece of paper in front of me. "Does this look familiar?"

It was a terrible, childish crayon drawing of an avocado, this one bearing a lopsided smiley face.

"It's a . . . bad avocado?" I said.

"It's a *happy* avocado!" they said, and tore the drawing to shreds. "God!" They tore the shreds into smaller shreds.

"Would it absolutely kill you to say *happy* avocado? Or is saying happy avocado something that's simply beyond your capacity?"

"Happy avocado," I said.

"Don't say it if you don't mean it," they sneered. "Don't patronize us." They took the shreds and rolled them into little balls and then tucked the little shreds inside their shirt pockets, carefully, as if for safekeeping. "We know when we've been talked down to, don't we?"

I didn't know what to say to that. I could see sweat beading up on their foreheads. I could see their shirts sticking to their chests. I began to feel a little sorry for them. "Listen," I said, "I think this has all been a big misunderstanding."

"Big misunderstanding?" they said.

"I mean, about the interview."

"Go on," they said. I could see them beginning to smile, just barely.

"Well," I said, "the thing is—"

"Yes?" they said. They gave me a hopeful, expectant look.

"The thing is," I said, "this whole thing is really about the Rita fiasco."

Their smiles widened. "The Rita fiasco? Aha. We thought you'd never mention it." They rubbed their hands together. Their teeth gleamed. "Anything else?"

"You bet there's something else," I said. "How about the way Corey has been acting lately? Or what's been happening with the green felt? Or Mr. Ditterhorn's habit? Don't tell me you didn't think I wasn't going to mention Mr. Ditterhorn's habit."

By this time, I could fairly see tears of joy forming at the corner of their eyes. But I had so much more to say, about Abigail's prophecies, about the customer service aura, about the idiotic hangnail policy, about why no one ever wanted to talk about the chameleon anymore.

They rehired me on the spot. I'm in sales now. Low sixes.

The Rooms

The children went to their rooms more often now, their parents noticed, without really noticing either. The parents had things to do, after all.

"Like what?" the children would have asked, in their pre-room phase.

"Adult things," the mother would have said, returning to her tablet, where bright and glittering candy awaited her clever swapping.

"Grown up things," the father would have said, frowning into his new cell phone. Why had he gotten this new cell phone anyway? True, his old phone didn't have as much data or memory, but it did fit easily into his pocket, while this new one was a real bear to carry around.

"A *real bear*," the mother sighed. "You say the same things, over and over."

"What were you saying?" the father asked. He was trying to recall his new passcode, which had two extra cockamamie digits in it.

"I said why don't you go upstairs and check on the children?"

"That's more like it," the father said. It was 5-8, his old high school football number.

Upstairs, the father found his son in his bedroom, watching videos on his laptop. He had headphones on, which made him look like either a child playing with headphones or an adult wearing headphones, the father couldn't tell. His son gave him a pitying smile. Probably watching something he wasn't supposed to, the little sneak.

"You spend all day in this room," the father said.

His son removed the headphones. "Did you say something?"

"I said since when did you put a TV in this room?" A giant flat-screen TV hung from the far wall.

"Let me get you some water," his son said.

The father said, "You should see yourself, wearing those."

His daughter was in her room, drawing butterflies or designing houses or doing taxes or making those little plastic headbands with the sequins the father could never figure out how to glue on right. And then to find them in the carpet, months later—well, he'd about had it up to here with those sequins.

But when he knocked on his daughter's door, she said she was on a conference call; could he give her fifteen minutes?

"You'd better not be starting up again with those sequins," the father said, loud enough that the mother came upstairs and told him to pipe down.

"Pipe down!" she said.

Their daughter opened her door, a phone held to her ear. *Just one minute*, she mouthed, but the parents couldn't tell if she'd actually mouthed, *See my room?*

They did. A home office fitted out with a desk, computer, and printer. Shelves of important looking binders with thick black spines. Someone had switched out their daughter's bright jumpers for a dark pantsuit. Her hair was streaked with gray.

"I'm not picking up those sequins," the father said.

"Over and over," the mother sighed.

"Here," their son said and handed them each a glass of water. "Let's get you two back to your room."

When Everything
Was Brown

I don't know what to say about those photographs, the ones from the years when we lived in a brown house, drove a brown car, owned a cat and a dog—both brown—and seemed to be perfectly at ease dressed in brown at every holiday meal. Even the food in those pictures, upon closer inspection, also seemed to lean toward brown, heavy on bean casseroles, Salisbury steak, and French onion soup. All I can say is that that was fine with everyone back then, or so it seemed to me. No one said anything about it. It just felt like normal life, you know? You'd wake up for another brown day in your brown bed, pull your brown comforter across your brown pillows, brush your hair with a brown brush and wrestle a brown sweater over your head. That's just what you did. That didn't seem strange to anyone. No one minded if you climbed into your brown car and drove to a brown office building overlooking a brown park, brown leaves turning upon brown branches. No one noticed any of that. What would there be to notice?

It wasn't like you could *say* anything about it. Could you imagine that? Someone saying how strange it was that everything was brown? How would people react to that, even if it was true? Would they regret their brown loafers and sports coats? Would they feel oddly embarrassed to sit at a brown kitchen table fitted out with four brown chairs, each one topped with a brown cushion? What would you want them to *do* about it exactly? Hide their brown belts and brown corduroys from their neighbors, who, by the way, also wore brown and also dried their chins upon brown bath towels?

I guess what I'm saying is, it was hard to tell *in the moment* that everything was brown back then, even if that seems totally obvious now. Even if that's something we wouldn't do today. Unless, of course, we're totally doing something like that today, but we just can't notice, because we can't look back upon today yet, at least not for a little while. We'll need some time to pass, and then we'll be able to see the thing that we can't see now, whatever it is. And think how foolish we'll feel. God! We'll be amazed that no one ever noticed the thing that's so incredibly noticeable, the thing that will be without a doubt the first thing everyone in the future notices, because it is so painfully obvious. How could we not have seen it?

But here's the thing: I won't be embarrassed by it, whatever it is. I won't. Because what good would it do to be embarrassed? Nothing, that's what. So go ahead, take a picture. That's right. Get it all in. Everything in its embarrassing due. Because I was there when everything was brown, and I'm still here today when everything is whatever it is. See me smile!

Honey

I don't remember my first taste. The sweetness was just something that always seemed to be around, a part of everything I knew. I didn't question its presence in my life. Nor did I question my burgeoning habit. In those years I didn't find it strange to spend entire afternoons traipsing through the woods, alone, avoiding others, out searching for another drop. How I remember those days now, the feel of woodland breezes across my bare tummy, my shirt neglecting to cover my midriff, my legs guiding me through a landscape where each tree seemed to hold the promise of another hit, another success, another pot to clutch to my grateful mouth. The feel of the pot against my chest, ah! Although it embarrasses me now to think of my younger years, I do not regret my solitude, for I would like to think that those lonely afternoons shaped me, pointing me in the direction of the Self I have since become. Whoever that might be.

My earliest memories appear to me through a golden-toned lens, from my first impressions of my parents to my school days, where I excelled at nothing more than lunchtime, a well-packed pot awaiting me, enough sustenance to endure the hours until I could return home. I was not social, as they say; I did not make friends easily. Instead, friends found me. The ones I had, though, seemed wrapped up in their own miseries; they longed more for an audience to their unhappiness, perhaps, than genuine connection. One was hyperactive, boastful, and self-involved, bouncing from one egotistic enterprise to the next. One suffered undue anxiety, courtesy of a squeaky voice. Another was so besieged by depression and self-loathing that he took to wandering alone through the woods, eating thistles, as gloomy a proposition as I could imagine. I drank many pots to chase the image away.

A secret: It isn't the sweetness alone that attracts me. Something else draws me in. A kind of excess I anticipate and look forward to. Like the moment before plunging into a deep stream, the flow raising me up, buoying me to the surface, even as I spit water from my mouth. A rare sort of abundance that I can't seem to find anywhere else, although I've looked for it many times. I've looked in friendships, where my enthusiasm so often feels like a pose, a role I'm meant to play, to please others more than myself. In housekeeping, where my empty pots and jars collect like unrealized dreams. In foolish adventures, whose outcome is never in doubt. I long for a different journey. Interiority, inscape, to know what's hidden deep inside. That's the taste, when I lift the pot, remove the lid, and feel the nectar atop my tongue: the *inside*.

I am resigned to my habit; I do not plan to change. Gone are the days when I would give up the stuff for hours at a time—an afternoon, even—and once, during a summer thunderstorm whose sounds still haunt my dreams, an entire day. That day I endured my friends' empty banter and meaningless gestures for as long as I could stand it, until I discovered I could stand it no longer.

"Do you think you could stop it?" I said. "Just for once?"

"Stop?" they said. They'd been assembling a birthday cake from incorrect ingredients: old socks, ribbons, lilies, and twigs. "We thought you had oh so very much been looking forward to this."

"Well, you were wrong," I said.

"Wrong?" They nibbled their fingers nervously and raised their eyebrows theatrically. "We know you do so ever much enjoy decorating the happiest of happy birthday cakes!"

"It's no one's birthday," I said.

They exchanged frightened looks. Their limbs trembled and shook. "Oh," they said, "why, there's nothing happier than an especially fine everyday cake on an especially fine every day!"

"It's inedible," I said.

"Perhaps," they said, "you aren't feeling quite yourself at the present moment?"

"What I feel is what I feel," I said.

They exchanged glances. They mouthed words I could not hear. "We do so ever wish to see you feeling quite yourself again," they said. "That's something we wish more than anything." And, before I could object, one hopped atop the other's shoulders and reached for a pot, high on my kitchen shelf. When they swayed beneath the pot's surprising weight, the lid made a juddering noise. "Here," they said, and handed the pot to me. "To feel quite yourself again."

What can I say? I raised the pot to my lips and drank. Nectar ran down my chin, my shirt. I tasted the sweetness I've known my whole life, and yet I felt I tasted something new, some territory not yet explored, some mystery yet unsolved. For the first time, I looked inside the pot as I drank, a glimpse of myself, golden and gooey, eclipsed by shadow. Who was this looking back at me? I lifted the pot higher and drank deeper, hungrily, eager for knowledge. As I studied my reflection more closely, I understood that there was a part of myself that would always remain unreachable, no matter how much I drank, or how earnestly I wished to grasp it, and that, although I could perhaps one day understand that part of myself, the effort would be something of a bother.

Today You Are Green

This summer you turn thirteen, and what is a thirteen-year-old girl to be happy about? Don't ask your father, who turns to you now, standing before the mini-golf cashier, and asks, "Which color do you want to be?" Don't ask your father's girlfriend, who selects the yellow ball, an offbeat choice, with red, blue, and green still in the offing, and gives you a playful nudge, the way she sometimes does, to signal that she knows how you must be feeling. But how do you feel? Several contradictory options present themselves. Best bet is to select the green ball, a color that nearly blends in with the artificial grass. An idea that suddenly appeals to you.

"I'll keep score," your father says. He's already writing your name on the scorecard with a pencil the length of a spent cigarette. "You can go first," he says, too brightly, a sign that he's nervous about today, a return to the same mini-golf course you've always gone to, every summer, when your family rents the same beach house, but never since your parents split, and never with your father's girlfriend, who is several years his junior, and who used to work in your father's office, and who used to make you mix tapes to take with you to the beach house, and isn't it strange how some things work out?

At the first hole, an embarrassingly easy bank shot against a hippo's side, you manage to guide your ball into a water hazard nonetheless, while your father fails to bank his shot cleanly and must give in to the minor humiliation of straddling the hippo's tummy on his follow-up. Your father talks to himself in third person, the way he does when he's stressed, saying, "Come on, Bob, you're better than this," and, "Bob, use your head," and, "Think, Bob, *think*." Your father's girlfriend takes one practice swing, then expertly ricochets her shot off the hippo's leg for an easy tap-in. You finish the hole with a duffer's four, not taking a penalty for the water hazard. Your father scribbles his score on the sly.

The thing is, you loved those mix tapes. Those tapes were like an introduction to being cool, although you would never admit that to your father's girlfriend now, no, not with everything that's happened since. But still. You've listened to those tapes a thousand times. You've got whole sides memorized. Today it occurs to you that this year you won't get a mix tape, a realization that makes you feel sort of sad in a vague, empty, shapeless way, the way so many things do these days. Most nights, you cry in private, for reasons that still aren't clear to you.

"It's your turn," your father says on this, the third hole. What happened to the second? No matter. This one is

Western themed, with a pesky wagon wheel that lures your green ball into one of its spokes. Your father talks his way through a cattle yoke—"That's more like it, Bob"— but whiffs on an easy tapper and ends up with a lowly four, while your father's girlfriend sails by the wagon like it's not even there, and cups out of a potential hole-in-one.

"Oh! So close!" your father exclaims, forgetting to hide his relief.

"Yeah," your father's girlfriend says, then taps the ball in with her flip-flop.

"So, let's see," your father says as he scribbles down the score, "that would be a two."

On the fifth hole, you somehow manage to cross a drawbridge and walk away with a three, your best hole of the day.

"Nice shot," your father's girlfriend says.

"Thanks," you say.

"Just keep lightening up that touch," she says, without further explanation.

On some of the tapes, she would record little secret greetings, five second hellos, or short introductions to the next song. "This next one," she'd say, "is a reminder why you don't actually need boys in your life." Here she had laughed, before the next song played, a song that had accompanied you all summer long, your favorite, the one you rewound a thousand times, the one you played so many times it got all mixed up with everything else.

On the ninth hole, your father sends his shot out of play and into a cluster of teenagers who congregate by a soda machine. "This yours?" one of them says, and then the rest of them crack up, like this is the funniest thing they've ever heard. When your father's girlfriend retrieves the ball, you can see the teenagers checking her out. Your father's girlfriend is pretty—beautiful, even. Your feelings on this subject are varied, warring, complex. The teenagers watch your father's girlfriend line up her next shot, whoop and applaud when she sinks a hole-in-one.

"Nice!" they exclaim. "Sweet!"

Your father makes an excellent shot, too, enough for a solid two, but you can hear him mutter, "That's not going to do it today, Bob," as he glumly retrieves his ball from the cup. The stupid necklace his girlfriend gave him, several years too young for him, dangles stupidly from his neck, but this time you don't want to tear it off and toss it into the surf, as you did this morning, when the three of you walked along the beach. This time you want to pull your father in for a hug. Another contradictory feeling, to keep all the others company.

Three disappointing holes later, your father's girlfriend is leaving you and your father in the dust. She doesn't acknowledge her second hole-in-one, nor do the teenagers, who lost interest awhile ago. You are hot and sweaty; your underarms stamp your T-shirt with embarrassing half-moons, the way they do more often now, drawing attention to you, you believe, despite a lack of supporting evidence.

"Do you two want to call it a day?" your father's girlfriend asks, out of charity or boredom or spite, who can tell?

"Never," your father says, intending playfulness. "No way."

Here is something you are glad no one knows about you: sometimes you get angry for no reason whatsoever, and then get even angrier at yourself for being angry for no reason whatsoever, until it is all you can do to lock yourself in the downstairs bathroom and look at yourself in the mirror, staring down the stranger there. Who is this person? you wonder.

At last, the eighteenth hole: the volcano. The hole where you've posed for a half dozen family photos. Hit the ball through the volcano's glowing core, then race across the rope bridge to the other side to see where it has disappointingly landed. The impossible hole. Now you each take turns, sending your shots through, and then for reasons that reveal themselves to you once you reach the other side, you sprint across the rope bridge to see that your father's girlfriend has hit yet another hole-in-one, while your ball shelters behind a lava obstacle and your father's ball rests in a water hazard. Quickly, you toss your father's girlfriend's ball into the water hazard and replace it with your father's ball, still wet, still glistening. "Hole-in-one!" you surprise yourself by shouting. "Hole-in-one!"

Your father's expression, upon crossing the bridge? Well, you will keep it with you a long while. Longer than the look your father's girlfriend turns on you as your father shakes water from his ball; now, how did that happen? Your mixed feelings take a little break, for once, which is nice of them. Otherwise you wouldn't be able to tolerate your father's childish smile.

The rest of summer? You spend your days wandering the boardwalk, to avoid your father and girlfriend's silent arguments. Eventually you meet a boy. You begin hanging out. He tries to kiss you and more and you let him, after a while. And so on.

How It All Fell Apart

They were all terrific friends—they were!—until they weren't. How often they got together and laughed and gossiped and flirted and cried and hugged and told each other about their lives, about what mattered most deeply to them. Although they never said it outright, they felt, in varying degrees, that they were somehow loved and accepted by one another. Admired, even. They believed that, were anyone to ask any of the others what they thought of them, that person would say without hesitation, "Oh, we *love* him (or her)!" Because that's how it was before it all fell apart, even though it didn't seem that way after. After, it seemed like hidden resentments and barely suppressed grievances that had always been boiling just beneath the surface of their conversations finally came to light, until there was nothing left to do but for those tensions to break through and run their natural course. Was that the truth?

At first it did seem like everything was nearly ideal. The friends got together for drinks or dinner or both, potluck meals or grilling on their new grills, which accompanied first houses and first mortgages. Dogs and puppies featured prominently in this era, always underfoot and

ready for another scrap of burger on the sly, when everyone else wasn't looking, off to get another beer. Beer and
more talk about beer, preferences, kinds, brews, new styles,
favorites, and standbys. How much of the early days
seemed a conversation fitted around another buzzy trip to
the refrigerator, an opener magnetized to the refrigerator's
side, the feeling of liberating the cap from the bottle's grip
a ritual that seemed to signal community, fellowship, and
togetherness itself. Or maybe everyone was just sort of
drunk? Who could say? Returning to the group, a friend
would find that two other friends had already gotten them
a beer on their last trip inside. They lined the bottles up at
their feet and drank them methodically, pleasurably.

The friends couldn't blame everything falling apart on
the babies. No, that wouldn't be fair. Because the babies
were adorable and beautiful, and made the get-togethers
and parties even more meaningful, if such a thing were
possible. The feeling of holding a sleeping baby in one
arm while bringing a fourth beer to your lips with the
other! They wouldn't trade that feeling for anything in the
world, would they? So it would be wrong to point a finger at the babies. Still, even though it wasn't the babies'
fault, they couldn't ignore that conversation began to
falter during the baby era. Listening to another parent's
exuberant, familiar experience of parenting was about as
pleasing as listening to someone else's breathless descrip-
tion of a vivid dream: *it was like I was in a train station, but*

I knew the train station was actually my childhood house, and my Aunt Vicky was sitting at a table waiting for me, which is weird because I've only met her once, when I was five. The friends listened and nodded. Laughed appropriately.

Afterward, they talked in private, on the drive home.

Do you think M_____ had a good time tonight? they said.

I guess so. Why?

I don't know, I thought she seemed a little mad at me.

Mad? Why would she be mad at you?

Maybe not mad. Maybe bored. She kept checking her phone while I was talking to her.

M_____ always does that.

Well, she never does that to me.

Really? She's done that to me ever since I said that thing about B_____.

Well, you shouldn't have said that thing about B_____.

I know.

Lately it's like I think everyone is a little bit mad at me.

Eventually, the friends sensed each other's anger without acknowledging it, enough that, over time, each other's anger began to feel normal, expected. Or maybe it didn't happen that way at all? Maybe no one was angry at anyone, really; maybe they were just busy, occupied with parenting and careers, trying desperately to strike the proper pose of responsible adults. Or did they just drink less now, and noticed, without the fog of alcohol, that they'd never really liked each other as much as they wanted to, or had pretended to? Or, let's just say it: maybe it was the babies' fault. No, never. Even though one friend said, on the drive home from another listless party, I've never felt more different from anyone in my life than the way I feel around people my age with children.

Maybe they would never know how it all fell apart. Only enough to say that yes, it did. It all fell apart. There. Perhaps they would feel wise about it one day, once they had some perspective. And wasn't it true that, with each passing day, how it all fell apart emerged further from the shadows and moved gradually into the light? Yes. The thing was, they imagined, in time, they would eventually understand how it all fell apart, but, by that point, they probably wouldn't care anymore.

So Much

When had "thank you" been replaced by "thank you *so much*"? The parents didn't know. How would they know? They had been too busy getting married, having children, finding jobs, moving from one place to the other, until they'd settled down, their children older, their jobs relatively secure, to keep their marriage company. Somewhere in there, "thank you" had become "thank you *so much*," without either of them realizing it. They heard it on the lips of sales clerks, cashiers, waiters, servers, customer service representatives, and telemarketers, whose numbers had dwindled during the years they'd spent becoming responsible adults. Whatever happened to telemarketers? Probably the same thing that had happened to "thank you," the parents figured.

There had been other changes, the parents agreed. Grocery bags, which they'd both secretly liked for their sweet inner scent of pulped paper, had been replaced by canvas sacks, which they sometimes left in the car for weeks, and which sometimes acquired the smell of rotting fruit. Bottled water, which they had drunk proudly, liberating themselves from soda and lemonade, had yielded to reusable water bottles, which they lugged around like the rest of the world, and which never fit quite right in their cars' cupholders. Compact discs were gradually eclipsed by MP3s and then MP3s were suddenly eclipsed by Spotify, which seemed to offer almost too much—who needed all of that?—as quickly as their wristwatches were replaced by smartphones; handier, sure, but farewell to the pleasure of raising their wrists impatiently and checking the time, in perfect approximation of someone in a rush. Which they weren't. But still.

"Mom, Dad," their children said. "No one watches cable TV anymore."

"How do they watch the news?" they asked.

Their children smiled at one another, exchanged knowing looks. "They don't," the children said, "they just check their phones."

"The screen is too small," claimed the parents, who still preferred the evening news, its usual horrors now playing across the seventy-inch flatscreen that had replaced the forty-two inch that had replaced the thirty-inch, years ago, when "thank you" was still socially acceptable. Those seemed like the good old days now, didn't they? After all, what was wrong with "thank you"? It said exactly what it meant. No filler. No wasted words. What was it about "so much" that seemed to appeal to everyone, for whatever reasons? Wasn't the addition of "so much" a clear sign that the "thank you" that preceded it might be in doubt, insincere, in need of reinforcement? In a way, didn't "so much" undermine the entire enterprise of thanking someone in the first place?

"Oh, Mom and Dad," their children laughed. "You just don't get it."

"Don't get what?" the parents said.

"Don't worry," their children said; they still loved them. So much.

The Same Snow

Although no one knew it but Connor, today's snow was, in fact, the same snow as when he was a kid. The same, exactly. There was no mistaking it, really. Those fat flakes yielding, by midafternoon, to smaller ones that seemed to drift both upward and downward at the same time, the upward drift creating, between houses and alleyways, sudden mists that vanished as quickly as they appeared: he'd remembered those. Yes. And when he'd stepped from his front porch to the walkway, the snow yielded to accept the width of his boots, just as it had done before. His hands, gloveless, ached. His breath plumed nostalgically before him. For a moment Connor stopped and looked up at the sky, as he had done when he was a kid and had first seen this snow, returned, after all these years, for whatever reason. Why had it come back? What news did it have to bring? Snow, indifferent to his questions, caught wetly in his eyelashes.

Connor was late for his haircut. The stylist greeted him from the back of the salon, where she'd been smoking, no doubt, the back door propped open with a trashcan, admitting a view of the shopping center, where the same snow was steadily falling.

"So, what were we thinking of today?" the stylist asked after she'd tied a too-tight cape around his neck.

"Same as always," he said.

"Same as always," she said. "Sounds good."

They talked about the weather. The stylist said she couldn't remember it snowing this early in the year before. Connor said it used to snow this early, when he was a kid. The stylist said that's right, she knew what he meant; it *would* always snow earlier when she was a kid. Wasn't that the truth?

"Right," Connor said.

"You always love it," the stylist said, "when you're a kid."

Connor had been seven years old the first time he'd seen today's snow. That was the year his parents split, the year his father moved across town, into an apartment strangely furnished with thrift-store finds and curbside hauls, while Connor and his mother stayed behind, in the same house he had ever known. School had been canceled that day, and his mother, who normally had to rise a half hour before him to get ready for her shift at the supermarket, had stayed home, unable, she discovered, to start her car. She'd returned to bed, while Connor went out into the snow without asking, for what seemed the first time ever, permission to do so. Why did anyone need to ask permission anyway?

He'd dressed himself in his winter scarf, coat, and gloves—he forgot his hat, but the coat was hooded—and opened the front door. A small snowdrift, loosely wedged against the doorstep, collapsed into the foyer. Outside, the wind seemed to pick up the moment he stepped from the front porch to the lawn, which still held the shape of the flowerbed. He pulled up his hood, which was already freckled with snow. His ears burned.

When Connor reached the driveway, he saw his mother's car still there, her footprints barely visible, as were the marks she'd left on the front windshield from where she must have tried to clear the snow away. It made him sad to think about his mother clearing the snow before trying to start the car. His toes, improperly dressed in school socks, not winter wool, began to feel numb. It occurred to him that no other children were outside yet; he was now alone in a way he had never been alone before. For the first time in his life, no one had any idea where he was or what he was doing. His father was across town. His mother was asleep. His neighborhood was empty. Connor stood in the snow and sensed a new kind of loneliness, unknown to him all these years, revealing itself now. But there was no fear or disappointment in its discovery. Instead, he felt as if someone had placed a knit cap upon his head and carefully pulled it over his ears.

A moment later, a car passed by, breaking Connor's solitude. But not before he'd observed the special quality of this snow, its distinctive look, its ordinary yet unforgettable qualities. Its temporary offer of consolation.

Back inside the house, Connor pried his boots from his feet, which hurt a little. When he removed his socks, hard-packed snow the shape of loose knots fell to the floor.

It was still snowing by the time Connor left the salon. The snow seemed to be falling from the opposite direction now, but that was no matter; he recognized it anyway. It had done the same thing the moment after he had turned from the driveway and walked back to the front porch, to the front door, to the foyer, where the sudden warmth informed him he'd been underdressed the entire time. How foolish he'd been, out in the snow with no one watching. What was he thinking? The snowdrift he'd let fall into the foyer had puddled in his absence. He would have to clean it up before his mother saw it.

Now, all these years later, Connor crossed the parking lot, the same snow falling around him again. The lot was quiet, nearly empty. The same snow was back, here to tell him whatever it wanted him to know. Connor tucked his hands inside his pockets. This time, he decided, things would be different. This time he would understand.

The First State

In Delaware, it is illegal to slide on ice. Children live in fear of being caught, dare one another in wintry parking lots and snowy playgrounds. "You first!" the children say, to the other children, who say, "No, *you* first!" These exchanges can last for hours, days. The children's breath plumes before them. Their feet ache.

In Delaware, shoppers do not chat with cashiers. Sales are strictly a business transaction, nothing more. The shopper places his or her items in front of the cashier. The cashier says, "That's $47.33." The shopper sighs, as if aggrieved, put upon. The shopper wishes to suggest, through an exaggerated search for their credit card, not only that the price is too high but also that it is somehow probably the cashier's fault. The cashier knows this. That's why the cashier does not say "thank you" or "have a nice day" when the shopper takes the bags from his or her hands and stomps away.

In Delaware, it is not appropriate to compliment someone on their new hairstyle. When someone gets a new hairstyle, you are to say, "What the hell happened to your hair?"

In Delaware, the summers are relatively mild, but this is never to be mentioned. Summer is only to be spoken of as hot and humid, in that order. Only. So if Delawarean A says to Delawarean B, "Jesus, it's so hot and humid today," Delawarean B is then to say, "It's supposed to be hot and humid all week." Delawarean A then has the option to say, "I'm getting pretty sick and tired of how hot and humid it's been lately," since the phrase "sick and tired" is another approved expression, along with "about had it up to here" and "the hell with this."

In Delaware, there is no sales tax. $4.99 means four dollars and ninety-nine cents, period. Hand the cashier a five dollar bill and the cashier will hand back one penny. Delawarean's pockets are heavy with pennies. You can hear them jingle from across state lines. Maryland, for example.

In Delaware, drivers keep their license plates for life. All the license plates you see in Delaware are the ones the drivers got on their sixteenth birthday. That's why some of them look so scratchy.

In Delaware, no one likes to travel outside the state, since traveling outside the state invariably means meeting someone who will ask where the Delawarean is from, and then the Delawarean will have to hear the person from another state say, "You're the first person from Delaware I've ever met!" Say this to any traveling Delawarean, and the Delawarean will immediately stick their hands in their pockets and look away. Listen for the sound of pennies shuffling quietly, angrily.

In Delaware, on December 7, 1787, Delaware became the first state to ratify the Constitution. For one glorious day, Delaware was the shining star of the colonies, the embodiment of American idealism and enlightenment, the center of democracy itself. Then the next day happened, and it was back to the usual.

In Delaware, the appropriate way to order your food is by saying "I'll take," as in "*I'll take* the shrimp scampi" or "*I'll take* the crab cake sandwich" or "*I'll take* the house special." It is not appropriate to say "I'd like" or "I'd like to have" or the needlessly formal "I would please like to have," as is customary in other, friendlier states. Iowa, Minnesota, and Ohio, for example. Say "I would please like to have the chicken parmesan" to any Delawarean waiter and you will find yourself on the receiving end of a withering stare reserved especially for out-of-state diners. Out-of-state diners can expect their entrée to arrive late, underseasoned, and cold.

In Delaware, no one talks about their job. A job is just a job, a means to a paycheck, something to be endured. Do not try to engage a Delawarean about his or her job. Approved conversation topics: how hot and humid it is, this traffic we're having, it's like you can't get a decent tomato anymore. What the hell happened to your hair?

In Delaware, a tornado will occasionally form in the sky but will be driven away by the sheer power of Delawarean's collective complaints. During tornadoes, tens of thousands of Delawareans will stare outside, saying into phones pressed to angry heads, "Jesus, would you look at all these stupid clouds?" To date, no tornadoes have touched down in Delaware.

In Delaware, it is possible to casually drive through three states—Delaware, Maryland, and Pennsylvania—without even realizing which state you are in. Corollary: for out-of-state drivers, it is possible to drive through Delaware without ever realizing it, and to claim, upon meeting a

Delawarean who likely knows better, that you've never been to Delaware.

In Delaware, every citizen has the same exact dream every night but never discusses the dream with anyone else, and thus never discovers that others share the same dream. In the dream, a smiling dolphin figures prominently.

In Delaware, no one stops by. Stopping by is seriously frowned upon. A felony, in some counties.

In Delaware, to go to the beach is to *go down shore*, no matter which direction one is actually driving from. On all roads, from all compass points, people driving to the beach are, in fact, all *going down shore*. As in, "I talked to Helen and Jim last night; they said they were *going down shore* tomorrow."

In Delaware, everyone knows they will never be truly understood. To be a Delawarean is to be a kind of mystery to the rest of the country. It is useless to try to explain Delaware to a non-Delawarean. It's not even fun to try.

The Clock Museum

The children do not remember the Clock Museum. The Clock Museum was dull, boring, a snore. To visit there, as the children did more times than they realize, was something to be dreaded, like pop quizzes or the end of summer vacation. So who can blame the children if they can't recall the permission slips they were required to ask their parents to sign, or the shuddering bus that ferried them to the Clock Museum's unimpressive parking lot, where their teachers divided them into groups of two before ushering them to the museum's front steps? The children wore bright T-shirts for the occasion, a field trip ritual, as were the bag lunches the children dropped, one by one, into long coolers choked with ice.

In the lobby the children were greeted by the elderly couple who ran the museum, Mr. and Mrs. ____, but who can remember their names? Mr. and Mrs. ____ were the oldest people the children had ever seen. Older-than-grandparent old. The kind of old not reported anywhere in the children's news of the world, in TV or movies or books, or, as Mr. and Mrs. ____'s silver teeth and sunken posture would have them know, in their imaginations. The couple told the children the tedious story of the museum's history—the oldest clock museum in the world!—as the children fidgeted, snickered, and endured their teachers' admonishing *shhhs*. The children glanced at priceless clocks with the same looks they afforded canned goods. The children listened to the story of the master clockmaker, whose home this museum once was, as if the elderly couple had opened the dictionary to a random page and begun reading it aloud. So much nothing had happened in the world before the children arrived to enliven it.

Mr. and Mrs. ____ led the children into a room where tall clocks were encased in glass displays. They invited the children to get as close as they would like to the "timepieces" without touching the glass. If the children touched the glass, poor Mrs. ____ was going to have to spend the whole evening cleaning, Mr. ____ said, and flashed his silver teeth. The children wouldn't want poor Mrs. ____ to spend the whole evening cleaning, would they? The children leaned closer anyway, their T-shirts reflecting the display's wan glow, although the children would not remember this. If the children remembered anything at all, it was when Mrs. ____ held up a finger, as if to say "wait a moment," and then all the clocks chimed together in unison. Mrs. ____ closed her eyes and smiled.

But why did the children have to visit the Clock Museum at all? Clearly there were better options, like the pretzel factory, where you got to eat all the free pretzels you wanted, or the apple orchard, where they plied you with warm cider and apple donuts and let you run wild along the orchard's bee-drunk avenues. Even the art museum had a gift shop where you could buy those tiny snow globes that glittered when shook, until all the snow settled depressingly to the bottom. If the children were to learn why they must visit the Clock Museum, they would discover that it was the town's collective guilt that compelled them there, an apology for the town's indifference to that listless place, a penance for all of their parents' forgotten field trips to the museum, and for all the occasions the townspeople had driven by the Clock Museum and thought, *Who would ever want to go there?* It was also free.

Because the children did not know why they must visit the Clock Museum, and because they would later struggle to recall much about it, they did not remember the last room. The last room—the former workshop of the original owner, Mr. and Mrs. ____ told them as they entered—was cooler than the others, windowless and dim. Mr. ____ instructed the children to gather 'round the lone clock in the center of the room, whose large, metallic hands were open, free from enclosure. Had the children better recollection of what happened next, they would have found it strange that Mr. and Mrs. ____ enjoined them to put their hands upon the clock, whose face, the children would not remember, held, in lieu of numbers, the words DO YOU WANT TO TRAVEL THROUGH TIME? If only they could recall the feel of their fingertips upon those hands. If only they could remember the moment Mr. ____ instructed them to push or pull the hands in either direction they wished. In the darkness, Mr. ____'s teeth dimly gleamed. The children put their fingers to the hands, pulled and pushed, pushed and pulled.

At lunchtime the children's teachers spread blankets across the Clock Museum's weedy lawn. The teachers told the children to select their bag lunches from the coolers, but when the teachers opened the coolers, they found that the ice had melted to water, or had disappeared altogether. How had the ice melted so quickly? Had the water evaporated? The children fished out their soaked or soggy lunches, peanut butter and jelly sandwiches stale inside Ziploc bags, baloney and cheese furred with green and gray mold. What had happened to the sandwiches while they were in the museum? How long had the children been inside? How was it possible that, with such a monotonous tour through such a boring museum, the children seemed to have lost all track of time?

Cake

But where did the cake come from? The boy didn't know. Wrapped inside a piece of wax paper, the cake had been hidden in the back of the family freezer, deliberately, it seemed, behind the ice trays, where it remained for years. A tiny slice, barely three or four bites. Through the paper, the icing appeared thick, unappetizing. Why did someone go to such lengths to preserve this cake? Who would want it?

The boy asked his father.

His father said, "Don't ask me about the cake." He was doing the crossword on his cell phone while watching baseball on TV, the way he sometimes did. He had his feet on the coffee table; the boy could see holes in his socks. The holes made his father's socks look like puppets.

"But," the boy said.

But his father didn't say anything. He made the face he made whenever the crossword had gotten the best of him.

The boy asked his mother.

His mother told him he wasn't to touch the cake, ever. Would he promise her that? Please?

"Why?"

Because it was special cake, his mother said. She turned a smile on him that wasn't really a smile.

"Special, how?" the boy asked.

But his mother didn't answer him. She ran the dish disposal and the kitchen faucet at the same time, which was just about the loudest sound in the house, unless you counted the car starting up in the garage, which the boy didn't.

Time passed. The boy grew older. Taller. Able to reach all the way inside the freezer whenever he felt like it, which wasn't often. The boy's parents grew stranger, more mysterious. The boy's father took to staying up late at night, watching the news, the TV muted, the family room suffused with blue-green light. His mother bought a kind of bicycle that did not move, upon which she pedaled furiously, the bike's screen commanding her to go faster, faster. His mother obeyed, as if trying to escape. Whenever the boy thought he'd figured out something about his parents, it was like shining a flashlight down into the basement: one part was brilliantly revealed, but the rest was in shadow.

One day, the boy opened the freezer and looked for something to eat. The boy pushed aside frozen vegetables and fish sticks, pizzas wrapped in cellophane. The boy moved one ice tray aside and then the other. Reached his hand deep inside the freezer. Lifted the cake from its hiding spot. Closed the freezer door behind him.

When his parents found him at the kitchen table, the wax paper open, dotted with crumbs, they asked him how could he? How could he? His mother began to cry. Her shoulders shook. His father's face turned red and raw. The boy said he was sorry.

His parents sat down beside him. They gave one another looks the boy wasn't sure how to read. And then his parents told him about the boy. The other boy. The first boy. The one who came before him. The one who didn't make it. They told him how there had been a funeral, and a reception. How there had been a cake.

The boy looked down at the wax paper, empty now, save for a few yellow crumbs and smears of cheap icing, and moved his tongue along his lips, his first taste of loss.

Custodian

$\bigvee$r. Fulton was the custodian at my elementary school. Mr. Fulton wore overalls and heavy work boots. If we heard heavy work boots echoing throughout the hallways, we would instinctively think, *That must be Mr. Fulton.* Mr. Fulton had a yellow bucket and a white mop. The bucket had wheels that creaked noisily when Mr. Fulton pushed the bucket down the hallways. If someone spilled milk on the cafeteria floor, Mr. Fulton would materialize from wherever and mop the floor with the white mop. Mr. Fulton was good at mopping the floor quickly. Mr. Fulton wrung the white mop into the yellow bucket and then put a sign where he'd mopped. CAUTION: WET FLOOR, Mr. Fulton's sign read.

"Slow down, Buster Brown!" Mr. Fulton would say if we were running through the halls.

"That all for you?" Mr. Fulton would say when we carried our lunch trays past him.

"Where's the fire at?" Mr. Fulton would say at the end of the school day when we pushed through the front doors, eager to escape school and head home, where we would invariably forget about Mr. Fulton altogether. Unlike our teachers, say Mrs. Reese or Ms. Winkel or Ms.

Katz, Mr. Fulton wasn't the kind of person we thought about at home. The only time we thought about Mr. Fulton was when we heard him in the hallway, or when he appeared with his bucket and mop, and then we'd think, *There's Mr. Fulton.*

Mr. Fulton smoked cigarettes outside the cafeteria loading dock. If we waved to Mr. Fulton while he was smoking cigarettes outside the cafeteria loading dock, Mr. Fulton would not wave back. Mr. Fulton did not smile. Each year, there was a picture of Mr. Fulton not smiling in the yearbook. CUSTODIAN, it said above Mr. Fulton's picture. Mr. Fulton mowed the school grounds with a green tractor that had enormous black tires. If Mr. Fulton was mowing the school grounds with the green tractor, our teachers would sometimes close the windows until Mr. Fulton had stopped mowing the school grounds, and then they would open the windows again.

One rainy day, we arrived at school to see Mr. Fulton standing in the parking lot, which had flooded overnight. Brown water rose to Mr. Fulton's knees. Rain fell on Mr. Fulton's overalls. Mr. Fulton held the white mop in his hands, the white part visible.

"You kids go on home," Mr. Fulton said. "No school today."

We watched as Mr. Fulton thrust the mop into the floodwater and moved it about, invisibly, beneath the brown water. Was Mr. Fulton really going to mop up all the floodwater? We watched him for a few moments, our hearts beating in our ears, and then we turned to leave, a free day off from school before us, and we ran home not thinking or wondering or imagining what life was like for Mr. Fulton.

Mean Moon

Last night I met the Mean Moon. It was watching me from behind my blinds, the way it sometimes does on nights when I can't sleep. I stood from my bed and walked to the window, ready to confront the Mean Moon, but it hid the moment I pulled the blinds. The sky was dark, empty.

"I saw you, Mean Moon," I said.

Outside the wind picked up. Branches swayed and rocked.

"Don't think I didn't."

Later that night, after I had finally fallen asleep, after I was in the middle of a dream about my high school girlfriend, whom I hadn't seen in years, and whom I'd always meant to keep in touch with but had somehow never contacted, I heard a sound from downstairs. A sudden, thunderous rumbling.

Isn't that your automatic garage door? my high school girlfriend said—and that's when I woke up and realized, in an instant, that the Mean Moon must be up to something.

Downstairs, I could see moonbeams shooting out from the door that led from my kitchen to the garage. The beams were fantastically bright. Piercing. When I opened the door, I was temporarily blinded. Tears sprang from my eyes, one after the other; I couldn't stop them.

"I'm not crying," I said into the brightness. "It's just that it's so bright in here."

And that's when I heard the Mean Moon's voice for the first time. "Good evening," the Mean Moon said. Laughed.

What did the Mean Moon's voice sound like? Exactly like what you'd expect. Except deeper.

A moment later I was able to see well enough to observe the situation: the Mean Moon had opened my automatic garage door and had sat itself down in one of the plastic Adirondack chairs I'd been planning to put out on the back porch once the weather got nicer, except the Mean Moon wasn't so much sitting in the chair as sort of lumping part of itself into it, while the rest of the moon stretched out into my driveway, into my neighborhood, and presumably up into the night sky—but it was impossible for me to see.

"You're going to break that chair," I said.

But the Mean Moon didn't listen. Instead it laid into me about all of my shortcomings, failures, and limitations. About everything regrettable I'd ever said or done. The Mean Moon told me what a difficult person I could be, thoughtless at times, and described the ways I had alienated those around me. The Mean Moon gave several examples. The examples were sharp and specific. Turns out, the Mean Moon had been watching me for years.

And I would have maybe agreed with the Mean Moon on a few points, if the Adirondack chair didn't break at that moment, dropping the Mean Moon to the floor.

"Sorry," the Mean Moon said.

"I tried to tell you," I said.

But the Mean Moon had already risen, back into the sky, watchful, observant, but maybe not so bright.

Teachers

Mrs. L, 2nd grade

Mrs. L kept a typewriter in the corner of the classroom. A typewriter for us, she explained, to use whenever we wished. For whatever we wanted to write. Letters, stories, poems, lists, thoughts, or even just words. Sometimes it's fun just to write words, Mrs. L said. She smiled when she said this. The typewriter—a manual typewriter, I know now but didn't then—was thirty years out of style, a hand-me-down or thrift store find. A black Royal with round keys that required us to press as hard as our seven-year-old fingers could press, fingers that had hitherto only pushed video game joysticks and reluctant buttons through the narrow apertures of church jackets. The pleasure of scrolling a piece of paper into the carriage. Typing a line and then having to hit the carriage back—thwack! The sound of that. Someone looking over your shoulder, eager to see what you were writing. Wanting the other person to read what you'd written, and yet not wanting them to, either. The first time, feeling that.

Mrs. J, 3rd grade

On writing days Mrs. J would allow us to select one magic item from a plastic treasure chest she kept in the back of the classroom. The treasure chest was freckled with diamonds and rubies, also plastic, as was the flimsy lock and key. Inside: a ruby ring, a feather, a scroll, a seashell, a necklace, a gold leaf, an inkwell, a glass paperweight with a baby seahorse strangely encased within it. "These are magical items," Mrs. J explained, "to give you magical powers when you write." Choosing was difficult, unless you were toward the end of the alphabet, as I was. The scroll was the least popular item, which only served to enlist my affection for it all the more. A piece of red yarn held it together. Unfurled, the scroll was revealed to have an encouraging message written in calligraphy: *Use this on your writing journey.* Someone had blackened the edges of the scroll with a lighter, or, as I imagined it then, a pirate's torch.

Mrs. D, librarian, 4th grade

On library days Mrs. D would instruct us to gather in a circle in front of her desk. There she would read to us from one of the library's new releases, some mystery or fantasy or young adult novel. That we were a little too old for story-time escaped Mrs. D's notice; she loved reading aloud. She was good at it. Especially dialogue, which required her to adopt different voices and then remember those voices as the story developed. Still, we made fun of her later, at lunch. We imitated the way Mrs. D read aloud. We tried to make our voices sound the way Mrs. D made her voice sound when she read the dialogue. It was fun, trying to do that. Our secret: it thrilled us to feel the dialogue on our tongues. A first taste of language as pleasure, entertainment. Wanting to engage a listener. Wanting them to hang on our every word.

Brother J, 7th grade

In Brother J's religion class, we had to keep a yearly journal to record, he said, our thoughts and spiritual reflections. Our journals: spiral notebooks festooned with stickers, doodles, band logos, the Stones' lips and tongue, Led Zeppelin's cryptic insignia. We carried the journals home on weekends, neglected to write anything in them. Sometimes weeks passed with no thoughts or reflections whatsoever. "I will be collecting your journals at the end of the semester," Brother J said, "so please make sure they are up to date." He gave us a knowing look. Up to date: we invented thoughts; we fabricated reflections. We filled in blank days and weeks with sudden memories, recollections, observations. A realization: it's fun to remember things you can't quite actually remember, and then write them down as if you did.

Ms. K, 10th grade

Ms. K was our English teacher, there, ostensibly at the front of the classroom, to instruct us on diagramming sentences, grammar, punctuation, and the block paragraph business letter, but more often to read aloud her original poems and ask us for feedback. "What do you think?" she'd say after reading us another poem. Most of her poems were about motherhood. Ms. K had a young daughter, whom she sometimes brought to class, and whom Ms. K allowed to draw on the chalkboard in the middle of class while we were pretending to diagram sentences. We didn't know what to say. What did we know about poems, about motherhood? "I'm still looking for a title," Ms. K would say. "Sometimes I have a hard time figuring the title out." We raised our hands. We offered suggestions. "These are all good ideas," Ms. K would say, reaching for a piece of chalk. "I'd better write them down." I raised my hand. Ms. K called on me, and I listened to hear whatever it was I was about to say.

Better

It doesn't get any better than this, the parents agree: their children grown, married, off to start their own lives, while the parents finish up on theirs. *Mom! Dad! Don't say that!* their children say. But the parents aren't listening; they're off to the nursery again, to buy more trees. Then off to the new Mexican restaurant they don't really like but keep recommending to friends nonetheless, because if there's anything better than finishing a long day of tree planting with a sugary margarita and a second basket of flavorless chips, the parents don't know what it is.

Have you two considered a retirement community? the children ask. *You might really enjoy it. So many activities. So many groups to join!*

The parents don't actually carry the trees themselves. They pay a neighborhood boy to do it for them. Kevin. Or Ken. Either way, he's worth every blank check they've ever written him. The smile he gets whenever they hand him the check. The way he tries to hide it but can't. The parents love that about Kevin. Or Ken.

What a new tree lacks in shade, it more than makes up for in charm, the parents think. Branches raised, as if to ask *why*. And then to see the tree tugging against its ropes when the wind picks up, while the parents are on their way to pawn their children's bicycles at the consignment shop? Well, it doesn't get any better than that.

Please don't throw our old stuff out, the children say. *We still want those things. Please!*

The consignment store employees know the parents. Back again? they say. The parents show them what they've brought. The employees give them a look like, You two matter more to us than you could ever possibly realize.

It's amazing how much space has opened up inside the house since the children left. The parents can't believe it. Sometimes they wander through the hallways, carrying snacks they really aren't hungry for, marveling at the sound of their footsteps echoing through rooms once full of books and clothes and furniture. It's like finding another house inside the house. Or it's like being lost. Either way, the parents can see the new trees from the garage windows, now that the children's bicycles are gone.

One night the parents take some friends out to the Mexican restaurant. Our treat, they say. The friends argue, say they'll pay half, but the parents brush them aside. What's better than dinner out with friends? they say. They make menu recommendations. They direct the friends toward horrible dish after horrible dish. The parents order every terrible appetizer on the menu and insist on a pitcher of margaritas. A waiter wearing a black apron hands them each a heavy glass, rimmed with salt. They fill the glasses and then raise them for a toast.

What shall we toast to? the friends ask.

To this, the parents say. It doesn't get any better than this.

Nicotine

Babysitter says we aren't to hide her cigarettes again. Because hiding her cigarettes isn't funny, she says, but what we want to know is: Why can't we stop laughing? We give one another looks. Isn't it something, our looks seem to say, how we know where Babysitter's cigarettes are, and yet Babysitter does not? And what with Babysitter being so much older than us, and us being two kids who hid Babysitter's cigarettes in our mother's geraniums while Babysitter was in the bathroom. Babysitter says, "I'm giving you to the count of ten."

We clutch our sides, laugh.

"One," Babysitter says. She holds up a finger.

"Smoking is bad for you," we explain.

"Two." Babysitter holds up two fingers, the ones where usually a cigarette rests, the ash sometimes dangerously close to falling, even though it never does, not until the moment Babysitter expertly taps it into her Diet Coke can.

"We're trying to help you quit," we say. Which is the funniest thing we've said yet. The two of us, in our footie pajamas, helping Babysitter, who has streaky gray hair and drives a car with a window that's really a trash bag—imagine that!

"Three," Babysitter says.

We race upstairs. We sit on our beds, facing one another. Will Babysitter find her cigarettes in the geraniums? Maybe, if she thinks to open the front door and check the porch, where the geraniums preside, which she probably won't, because who would? Downstairs, we hear Babysitter opening kitchen cabinets.

"Five," Babysitter says. What happened to four?

"Not in the kitchen," we say.

We hear Babysitter walking heavily to the foyer, the way Babysitter sometimes walks, what with her ankles that are always giving her trouble. Babysitter opens the foyer closet, that familiar creak and sigh. The chime of empty hangers, the faint swish of riffled jackets and winter coats.

"Not the closet," we say. Does Babysitter hear?

"Six!" Babysitter says.

By the time Babysitter has opened the dining room breakfront and is reaching her hand inside our mother's porcelain pitcher, she is already at nine, and we are already back downstairs, watching.

"That's where we put them last time," we remind her. "We wouldn't do the same place twice," we explain helpfully.

Babysitter's expression is one that says she would just like to know why the world is conspiring against her, even when the world (us!) is just trying to help her quit smoking. "Sometimes I have no idea what you two want from me," she says, which is hilarious, since we already told her and since she will probably thank us one day.

But why does Babysitter tell us to grab our coats? "We're going on a little adventure," she says. But she didn't even count all the way to ten.

A little adventure: we sit in the back of Babysitter's car, which is crammed with plastic bags, crushed boxes, and cleaning supplies. From the back window that is really a trash bag, a nighttime breeze redolent of gardenias and car exhaust. In the passenger seat, an orange cat blinks disapprovingly at us from within a white carrier. The carrier wears a seatbelt. Who knew there was a cat in Babysitter's car this whole time?

"These are mean children," Babysitter says to the cat. "These are the meanest children in the world."

The cat, as if to agree, yawns, revealing its long, pink tongue.

We do not say a word. We shiver in the breeze. Headlights pass, one after the indifferent other.

At the gas station, Babysitter tells us to sit tight. We stare out the front window at a foreign country: a gas station at night, mosquitoes haloing the entrance, which swallows Babysitter up, then returns her a few minutes later, her labored gait easier now, her hands worrying the cellophane off a pack of cigarettes.

"Lookee what I found," Babysitter says, after she opens the car door and holds the pack to our faces. Babysitter's smile is crooked, embarrassing. Triumphant.

On the drive home, Babysitter lights one cigarette and then another. "When I was a kid," Babysitter says, "my mom would always say that it didn't take the littlest thing to be nice to another person." Babysitter exhales a plume of smoke that hovers over the cat, then dissipates out the window. "A whole lot easier than being mean."

We're not mean, we want to say; we're nice. But are we? The cat gives us a look, impossible to read. This is the latest car ride we've ever taken at night. Our hair acquires the smell of nicotine.

The following morning, we retrieve Babysitter's cigarettes from the gardenias. The pack has grown a skin of moisture overnight, but the cigarettes are dry, unharmed. We sneak them into our bedroom and hide them again, this time in our nightstand, underneath our diaries. We practice smoking, the cigarettes unlit.

"Darling," we say, our voices adopting British accents, "I simply adore your new hairstyle."

"Why, thank you," we say. "I quite adore it myself."

We eye one another, taking puffs from Babysitter's cigarettes, exhaling nothing into the air. This could be us, we think. This could be our lives.

My Lost Decade

My lost decade began in darkness. I opened my eyes and cried. Someone wrapped me in a blanket, striped pink and blue. A cap, several sizes too small, slipped from my head, which already sported thick dark hair. "Just look at that hair!" my parents said, as they passed me from one person to the next. "Gets that from his father," someone claimed. "No way," another contradicted. "That's his mother's hair if I ever saw it." Already my lost decade was marked by mixed reviews.

Time passed. I toured my house in a device shaped like a lily pad, from which my feet depended, somewhat uselessly, as they often steered me into the refrigerator, dishwasher, or the little fence strung across the top of the stairs. I spilled milk on the floor, soiled myself at dinner, and chewed a green rubber ring into a slobbery mess. I cried in the middle of church services, my parents whisking me away down the center aisle. "Shhhh," they whispered, but I knew they really wished to say, "Get yourself *together*, man. You should *see* yourself right now!"

Of course they put me in the institution.

Several, actually.

The first had a round carpet upon which we were to gather and listen to stories that offered curious instruction: Pop, it turned out, might enjoy it tremendously if we were to hop on him. A tall cat wearing a hat the approximate size of a barber's pole might just be our new best friend if only we let him inside when our parents were away. The foods we found most objectionable, repulsive, and disgusting were actually our favorites, if only we gave them a try.

The next institution was even worse. Each morning the other inmates cornered me in the locker room and whipped me with wet towels. Teachers spoke confusingly of "fractions" and "long division" and "studying." Report cards assaulted my personal notions of specialness. Chalk harangued my daydreams. After-school cartoons questioned the very value of homework itself. I reached out to fruit roll-ups and Yoo-hoo for guidance but finished them both before they could answer. My lost decade grew hazy and dim. My parents took me to see a man in a long white coat who asked me a series of bewildering questions, then imprisoned my eyes behind bifocals. I stared out anew at a world that had lost all sense and meaning, its perfectly clear signage notwithstanding.

I struggled socially. Friendships were fleeting during my lost decade. Everyone on the scene back then was tied to one another through the flimsiest of bonds: footwear choices, clothing allegiances, and snack preferences. We congregated in the cafeteria and laughed at things that weren't funny, our tongues brightened with Cheetos. We wanted to be seen, I suppose, in the wan glow of each other's spiritual emptiness. We sucked Juicy Juice from boxes impaled with sharp straws, adrift, searching.

At last my lost decade drew to a close. My parents sang a song and carried in a cake, ten candles flickering before me.

"Go ahead," my parents said. "Don't forget to make a wish."

I closed my eyes, my lost decade fading from view, and wished for the only thing worth wishing for: a comeback.

Long Distance

After my uncle died, he started calling me on his Kermit the Frog telephone. I was ten at the time, and kind of excited to have my own phone, even if it was my dead uncle's and even if he called me late at night, after I'd already fallen asleep.

"You awake?" my uncle asked.

"Well."

"Sorry," he said.

"That's okay," I said.

"Really?"

"Yeah," I said, even though I knew it really wasn't okay. But I didn't want my uncle to feel bad, what with him being nice enough to leave me his Kermit phone, and what with him being dead and all. Kermit phones were pretty cool back then.

My uncle told me what it was like to be dead, while I said things like "wow" or "really" or "that's so weird!" The things he said were observant and revelatory, even if I can't remember most of them now. You have no interest in remembering your life after you die—that's one thing I remember. Which surprised me. I mean, you would kind of think the opposite, right? My uncle told me about heaven, too, which he could describe in incredible detail. I've forgotten most of what he said, which I'm a little embarrassed about, but what ten-year-old pays attention to adults? There's a lake. In heaven, I mean. It's . . . big.

The thing is, whenever my uncle called, I was usually sort of asleep, which made it hard to pay attention. Plus I really got into the idea of being on my Kermit phone. I mean, I couldn't believe that I actually had my own phone, right in my bedroom, sitting on my nightstand, where I could call anyone in the world, if I wanted to, and anyone could call me. As my uncle told me about the afterlife, I'd twirl the phone cord around my finger, the way adults did on television, and stare into Kermit's ping-pong ball eyes. I liked to imagine someone walking in on me talking on my Kermit phone and feeling sort of jealous of me.

My uncle told me about my future. Things to watch out for. Things that mattered. Things he knew now that he was dead and in heaven, where, it turns out, they tell you stuff like that. That's another thing about heaven I forgot to mention earlier: you get to know everything about pretty much everything.

The Kermit phone stopped working after a while. First, the zero push button started sticking, and then the same thing happened with the three, until you couldn't dial any number with a zero or a three in it, which made it pretty useless.

I guess it didn't really matter. By that point my uncle had long since stopped calling me. He didn't give any explanation; he just didn't call anymore. Unless he did explain, and I wasn't listening.

You can't just walk up to celebrities or famous historical figures. There's a rule about it. They tell you day one.

My Money-Making
Scheme

I don't know what to say about how it all started, except to say that one day I was living paycheck to paycheck, counting every dime, and then the next day my wallet was bulging with tens and twenties. That's the truth. I know I should say I'm sorry, and I guess in certain ways I am, but the thing is, it was just so thrilling to have money in my pocket. For the first time in my life. When you've never had anything for so long, and then you have something, it changes you. It just does. It's like you've been living in darkness for as long as you can remember, and then someone hands you this, like, giant flashlight, and says, "Try this." And that flashlight is like, the biggest, brightest flashlight you've ever seen—well, that's a pretty special feeling.

I remember my first time. I was at the bank, signing my name across the back of another disappointing paycheck, when the teller remarked that I could deposit my check at the automated teller machine outside, which she referred to as an "ATM." Apparently, the bank had several of these, which anyone could use, any time of day or night. I could feel my heart beating in my ears.

"Thank you," I said, my tongue thickening with guilt.

Outside, I found the ATM encased in a glass kiosk that swallowed my "debit card" and then returned it to me, the kiosk door clicking open in what seemed a clear invitation to avarice. Inside: a whiff of damp shoes and newly minted fifties. My hands slickened in anticipation. The machine prompted me to insert my "debit card" and then asked for my "personal identification number," which I would soon privately come to think of as my "PIN," a little secret between the machine and me. I entered the number, whispering each digit aloud—but not too aloud. The machine gave me several options, one of which was, thrillingly, unbelievably, "withdrawal." I tapped the button and waited nervously. A moment later the machine spat out two twenties and a ten dollar bill, free for the taking. I hurriedly stuffed these into my wallet, where they seemed to fit perfectly, almost like my wallet had been designed for this very purpose. But it wasn't until I pushed through the kiosk door that I felt the full weight of what I'd just done: I'd entered with nothing in my wallet, and left with *fifty dollars cash, US legal tender.* Outside, the starry sky seemed to say, "Tell no one about this."

I didn't.

But my behavior grew worse. Soon I made any excuse to visit the ATM—the weekend's arrival, an upcoming birthday, my wallet feeling non-bulgy—and walked away with ever-increasing amounts: one hundred dollars, two hundred dollars, and once, the five hundred dollar maximum. I'd spend my profits at various shops and stores, the store owners eyeing my bills skeptically, then making change. "Here you go," they'd say, handing me back a ten or twenty, almost like they were waiting for me to confess.

"Thank you," I'd say, swallowing heavily.

Sometimes I'd visit the ATM in the early morning, sometimes at night. Never in the afternoon. I'd made a little ritual out of it, I guess, where the act of making the withdrawal was even more important than the money I was getting. That's something that feels important to say: it was always about something more than just the money. But it was also about the money, too.

I don't know how to get out. It's like they always say, it's a cycle that slowly pulls you in, little by little, until you've gotten in so deep that you don't even realize how deep you've gotten, the magnetic strip on your debit card wearing away to a frazzle. But here's the thing: on my last visit to the ATM, the machine refused my card. Spat it out like it was a fresh fifty, which it most definitely wasn't. "Insufficient funds," the message on the ATM's screen read. I peered closer to make sure I'd read correctly. The words glowed with accusation, malice. And maybe you can say I'm being naïve, and maybe you can say I have no idea which way is up, but when I read those words, it wasn't so much like I felt I'd been caught; it was more like I felt I'd been suddenly set free.

Tell Me and Tell Me True

It is the last day of summer vacation, which means the two friends have until tomorrow morning to annotate *The Odyssey*. They haven't started reading it, except for the first few pages, which are like, really boring. *The Odyssey* isn't one of those books you can get into. *The Odyssey* is one of those books people only pretend to get into, just to say they're into it. This is something the friends agree about. Like the way they agree that the Star Wars prequels are better than the originals because the lightsaber battles are more intense, or that LeBron James is seriously overrated, or that Christmas Eve is actually more fun than Christmas, since on Christmas Eve you still have Christmas to look forward to, whereas on Christmas it's like what do you have now?

The friends text one another throughout the evening. *How's it going?* they ask, or *Page?* One friend is on page 21; the other is on page 13. *Don't tell me what happens!!* the page 13 friend texts, and the other friend texts back *It gets so INSANE!!!* which they both know is a joke on account of the capitalization and exclamation points and on account of *The Odyssey* being *The Odyssey*. That's an important part of the friends' friendship: getting the joke. Another: never asking about each other's anxieties, fears, worries, hopes, or aspirations. The friends like to keep things simple, if you know what they mean.

The friends are required to use a specific annotation system. The system involves highlighters, gel pens, and sticky tabs. A yellow highlight refers to a MAIN IDEA; a pink highlight indicates THEME; and a green highlight means VOCAB. The gel pens are for margin notes, which should be brief, to the point, and unobtrusive. The sticky tabs are to remind the friends where they've made annotations, which is honestly just about every page, so why have the sticky tabs at all? That's another thing the friends joke about, the sticky tabs, which they call "sucky tabs." Sometimes they will say "sucky tabs!" in the middle of a conversation that has nothing to do with annotation, which is totally random and therefore hilarious.

By nine-thirty, the friends are on pages 68 and 45, respectively.

Reading The Odyssey is such an f-ing odyssey! one friend texts.

LOL! the other friend responds.

The friends haven't actually spent much time with one another outside of school, save for a few occasions when they've gotten together to work on projects or try out a new video game. When the friends play video games together, they talk only about the game, if at all, something neither of them finds strange. What else would they talk about? One friend's house is large, impressive, fitted out with tall windows that look out onto a landscaped yard; the other friend's house is tiny, a duplex, where the friend shares a room with a sibling, and the mother sleeps on a pullout bed.

Around eleven, the friends exchange another round of texts. *You awake?*

Hate. This. Book. one friend texts, and the other responds with an emphasized *HA!*

In school, the friends sit next to one another in class, or not. It isn't like sitting next to one another is a requirement of their friendship. Lunchtime, the friends sit at the breezeway tables, the least desirable seating in the café court. Sometimes they talk to one another, sometimes not. Sometimes the friends eat their entire meal without saying a word to one another, and that's fine with them. Afterward, they carry their lunch trays to the breezeway trash bins and silently divide recyclable from nonrecyclable garbage.

At 12:17 a.m., one friend texts *Just splashed my face with water.* The other friend texts back a face and water emoji, then adds a thumbs up, which they weren't going to include at first, but figures why not.

Once, when the friends were hanging out at the duplex house, the duplex friend's mother slept on the pullout bed the entire time they played a video game and didn't even wake up to say goodbye when the other friend had to go home to his tall-windowed house.

Here's what 2:00 a.m. would like the friends to know: it's hard to pay attention to *The Odyssey*, even with annotations. That must be why their teachers make them write annotations in the first place, to try to keep them interested. But the annotations are confusing, since a MAIN IDEA sometimes seems like a THEME and a THEME sometimes seems like a MAIN IDEA. Should they highlight those yellow or pink? Both?

The friends do not talk about some of the things they've observed about one another. That one friend has an odd way of pacing when nervous; that the other wears two T-shirts beneath a long-sleeved shirt even on warm days; that one pronounces "especially" as "ex-specially"; that the other once cried a little in the middle of a class presentation about dolphins; that neither of them seems to have any other friends besides each other.

So the friends read on, into the morning, long after they've stopped texting one another. Long after they've splashed their faces for the third and fourth times, fighting off sleep. Long after they've affixed their last sticky tab. Long after they've stopped wondering if the way life feels to them is the way it feels to the other.

Checking In

The family had been on vacation for only a day or two when the father realized he hadn't checked the refrigerator door before they'd left—a foolish mistake, an oversight that might cost them. Especially if the door, released from its magnetic hold, had swung open a few inches, the way it did the last time they'd traveled. They'd had to throw out everything that time. Lettuce, eggs, cheese, plus the holiday grapefruit the father had meant to toss weeks before. The smell had lingered for days, even after the father removed the refrigerator's cantilevered shelves and rinsed them in the sink. The father couldn't let that happen again. No. He would drive home and make sure the door was closed tight. A sensible decision. No harm, after all, in checking in.

The drive home seemed longer than he'd remembered, though. So many stretches of dull highways, bordered with trees the father didn't recall being bare, but maybe he hadn't been paying attention before? That happened sometimes. Especially on vacation drives, the father behind the wheel while the rest of the family slept, dozed, watched, listened, gamed, or did whatever it was they did with their devices while the father tried to find NPR again on the radio. He was good at that, finding one NPR affiliate after the other, although the family never noticed. They stared out the windows, expressions impossible to read, their ears sprouting AirPods.

The vacation hadn't been going well. The family visited an art museum, where the father seemed to have gotten lost during an audio tour, his family disappearing to wherever, while the tour guide's voice invited him to observe brushstrokes, color combinations, and skies swirled with stars. The father caught up with the family later, at a restaurant, but they already seemed to have eaten. The father said he would get something to go, but by the time his order was ready, his family must have already returned to their hotel. The father ate his meal on the walk back, taking bites of a wrapped sandwich and sipping tea from a strawless lid. That's what he'd been doing when he remembered about the refrigerator. He had decided, right then, to drive home and check. Certainly his family would understand.

The house was just as he'd left it, front door locked, window shades drawn tight. The father entered: a fragrance of darkened house, redolent of carpet, dust, absence. In the kitchen the refrigerator hummed and gleamed in the sudden brightness of overhead lights. The father approached, wrapped his fingers around the handle. And he was about to give the door a tug, to see if it really had been open this whole time, when he heard his cell phone ringing from his pocket, and knew, before he removed the phone and saw the caller's name on the display, that surely this must be his family, wondering where he was, worried, concerned, fearful, calling and checking in.

You Seem Like an
Interesting Person

My senior year of college, a woman I'd never met sent me a postcard, inviting me out for coffee. The postcard was a black-and-white photograph of Jackson Pollock crouching above a floor-stretched canvas, a thread of paint narrowing from his upturned brush, his lip wearing a cigarette. I'd seen the postcard before; you could buy several like it at the university bookstore where I worked for one semester and still sometimes loitered, hoping whoever was working the register would let me use my employee discount. I'd linger in the book aisles, browsing the first pages of novels I knew I'd never finish, even if I did end up buying them on discount and taking them home, where they joined all the other unfinished books on my shelves.

The woman's name was Leigh. Leigh was friends with my roommate, she explained, in her neat, smallish script, and she'd happened to see my room the last time she'd visited our apartment. Even though this wasn't the kind of thing she usually did, she decided to write to me and ask if I might like to meet for coffee sometime. Would I?

From what she had seen, she felt like we might have a lot in common. Books, music, art. She mentioned that she liked my paintings. *You seem like an interesting person*, she'd written before signing her name.

My roommate and I lived in an old townhouse that had been converted into apartments. My room, at the back of the house, looked out onto an empty field that doubled as a church parking lot. On Sundays cars materialized in the field long before I woke, their windows glossy in the morning light. I'd only taken the room because the former tenant had broken his lease, and my roommate needed someone in a hurry. My roommate and I knew each other through mutual friends but weren't actually friends ourselves, a small detail that became the largest one once my roommate began bringing his girlfriend's home. He had several. Sometimes I met them, if I made the mistake of sitting downstairs late at night, when he stumbled in. I'd wave a sheepish hello and then my roommate would say, "This is my roommate, Ned" as he and his friend ascended the stairs to his bedroom. "He's really into art."

I'd declared an art major my sophomore year, but two years later, I couldn't say why. My oil paintings were as listless as my watercolors, my sketches and figure drawings evidence of weak and weakening fundamentals. I'd chosen my major aimlessly, on the flawed belief that aimlessness was a prerequisite to greatness. One day, I believed, my talent, lying in wait all these shapeless years, would surprise me. Until then I would need to be careful to strike the right pose. To make it seem that the adulation that awaited me was as astonishing to me as it was to everyone else. I walked around campus in secondhand sweaters and ripped jeans, my Converse deliberately untied, waiting for the moment when the movie that played in my head would match the one that unfolded before me. I kept a pencil knife in my jeans pocket. I caught the campus bus, my sketchbook wet with rain.

But the moment never arrived. I showed up at my studio and worked on my mediocre art, or hung around with my friends, each of them more talented than me, and made self-deprecating jokes I hoped wouldn't be read as the pleas for praise they really were. I'd compliment my classmates' paintings, help them matte odd-sized sketches, give them unsolicited offers to help sell their work at local art fairs. Sometimes they gave me their paintings, just because, and I'd hang those paintings on my bedroom walls. Eventually, they took up my entire room. Still lifes, portraits, and abstractions well beyond my ability. On Sundays I'd hear the cars pulling out of the church lot, and, in the moment I awoke, it seemed that the paintings were truly mine. But then the moment would pass, and I'd be returned to the sound of cars driving off to wherever.

I waited a while before calling Leigh. We agreed to meet for coffee. What do I remember about the meeting? I remember thinking that Leigh was attractive, and then trying to steer the conversation in various ways so that it might lead to us sleeping together. But the conversation refused that path, mostly, as I later learned, because Leigh could see through my plan and knew how to derail it, even though I didn't realize it at the time. What did I realize? Not much, probably. Nothing beyond the kindness of the unfortunate woman before me, a person who had mistaken me for someone I wasn't. Once I grasped that we weren't going to end up in bed together, I thought about telling Leigh the truth, that I hadn't painted the paintings she'd admired, that I wasn't who she thought I was, that I wasn't an interesting person after all. But something held me back. I sipped my coffee and nodded politely. I failed to think of what to say.

But that's not how Leigh remembers it. What Leigh remembers is watching me enter the café and seeing me see her, the moment before I walked over and introduced myself. How uncertain I looked, how fearful. How I seemed to recognize that this was her, the woman who'd written the postcard, but didn't know what came next. "You were deciding which person you should be," Leigh says now, after twenty-one years of marriage together, two children, the eldest headed off to college in the fall. "I saw who you were," Leigh says, "and thought I could show you who you might become."

Just One More Time

Everyone asks the boy to do the impression. Still. Even now. Even after Mr. Martinelli died and no longer teaches at their school. Even with Mr. Martinelli being replaced by Ms. Link, whom the boy cannot seem to do an impression of, no matter how many times he tries to capture the way her sentences go up at the end, like she's asking a question, when all she is really doing is telling the class to open their textbooks to page 35. In a way the boy misses Mr. Martinelli, because Mr. Martinelli was so easy to impersonate, but that's a terrible thing to think; the boy must stop thinking it.

The boy's classmates follow him down hallways. They crowd him on the bus. They corner him at lunch, just as he is pretending to drink from his empty thermos and ask him to do his Mr. Martinelli impression. *Come on*, they say. *Do it!*

At first the boy resists, says he won't, tells them to leave him alone, but everyone knows he's just saying that. The boy is basically friendless, his impressions of teachers the only thing that keep him from falling off the cliff of respectability altogether.

Please, his classmates say. They sit next to him, put their hands upon his shoulders, feign care, interest. *Just one more time.*

So the boy does his Mr. Martinelli impression. He turns one side of his collar up, hunches his shoulders forward, raises an index finger, as if to make a point, and says, "Ah, gentlemen, I believe the show is, ah, up here, not outside the window, co-*rrect*?" He turns his gaze to the cafeteria lights, rests one hand against his cheek, says, "Your last papers had some, ah, holes so big that my mother-in-law could fit through them, and I can, ah, assure you that—"

She's quite a large woman! the boy's classmates say, laughing. *Oh my God! That's him!*

Here's something the boy is glad no one knows: he sometimes does his Mr. Martinelli impression when no one is around, just because. Like when he's walking home from the bus, where he will soon need to retrieve the housekey from the fake rock beneath the mailbox and turn it in the lock, his mom not home until five-thirty. The boy likes to have Mr. Martinelli comment on whatever he sees, as if observing it for the first time. "This really is a steep, ah, driveway, isn't it? One feels it, ah, most forcibly in the knees." The boy likes doing the impression, the way he can try out words he would never use in real life, like "quite" or "forcibly."

Mr. Martinelli died from cancer. The boy knows that. Everyone knows that now, but no one knew it back then, when Ms. Link began to sub for Mr. Martinelli. The boy didn't think anything about Mr. Martinelli missing so many classes. He kept doing the impression all through that time, something he can't decide if he feels bad about now. If only everyone would let him forget about the impression, he could maybe forget about doing it all those times when Mr. Martinelli was sick, and then he wouldn't have to decide whether or not he feels bad about it.

But they won't let up. His classmates keep pestering him. *Just one more time*, they say. Upperclassmen stop him in the parking lot. *You're the kid who does Mr. Martinelli, right? Let's hear it.* So the boy bends his collar, hunches his shoulders, exaggerates Mr. Martinelli's "ahs" and the upperclassmen laugh and laugh, even though they never talk to him again, not even when they see the boy in the cafeteria breezeway, where he usually eats with people he doesn't even know. The boy likes to imagine a scene where the upperclassmen stop to ask him to do the impression, and all the people he doesn't know are impressed, but the boy knows that's a dumb thing to imagine.

But here's something the boy is never going to tell anyone. Ever. One day, a few months before Ms. Link replaced Mr. Martinelli for good, the boy was leaving Mr. Martinelli's classroom when Mr. Martinelli asked to see him for a moment. The boy walked to Mr. Martinelli's desk, the air thickening around him, as the last students left the room. Up close, Mr. Martinelli's skin looked mottled and pale. A slickness clung to his eyes.

"I hear you do an impression of me," Mr. Martinelli said.

The boy felt his breath catch.

"I've heard it's quite, ah, accurate."

Heat surged through the boy's face, neck. "I'm sorry," he said.

"I'd like to hear it," Mr. Martinelli said.

And the boy would have said no, would have begged off, if Mr. Martinelli's expression hadn't informed him that he could not say no. So the boy did the impression. He did all the "ahs" and hand gestures. He made the joke about the mother-in-law. When he finished, it took him a moment to realize that Mr. Martinelli was smiling.

"That's quite apt," Mr. Martinelli said. "You've got a real flair for impressions." Then, "Keep up, ah, the good work."

Now, the boy plays those words over and over again. Did Mr. Martinelli want him to keep doing the impression? Even though he died? Even now? The boy can't decide. The boy looks forward to a time where people will stop asking him to do the impression, and then he won't have to think about what Mr. Martinelli said to him, or how Mr. Martinelli died, or how it was kind of fun to do the impression when no one was around. Pretty soon the boy won't have to think about any of that. Pretty soon life will be simpler, easier.

First Everything

The night Katherine lost her virginity, she went to a lecture with her boyfriend, Carlton. The lecture, a music professor's sabbatical presentation, was to be held in a recital hall, an empty, unremarkable room, save for the Baldwin grand yawning before them, its lid propped wide. Katherine didn't really want to go but had agreed anyway. Katherine was seventeen, a high school senior; Carlton was a year older, a college freshman and Katherine's former high school classmate. They had been dating for four months, Katherine making the thirty-minute drive to campus on most weekends. Now, Carlton led her to the back row, where he talked to her about his newly discovered admiration for Beethoven and Scriabin. Katherine listened, without quite listening either. She was getting better and better at that, she realized with some regret.

After ten minutes had passed, with no one else joining them in the audience, a janitor opened the recital hall's door and pushed a gray cart through the doorway.

"Is there a lecture here tonight?" Carlton asked.

"Not by me," the janitor said. The cart was fitted out with a broom, a mop, and the same kind of yellow rag

Katherine's father sometimes used to clean his ancient Pontiac Bonneville, Sunday afternoon yielding to evening as he coaxed the Bonneville's hood into an obedient shine. Katherine thought about her father now, waiting at home, telling her mother it was okay, she could go to bed now.

"I think maybe we should leave," she whispered.

"Okay," Carlton said.

As they were leaving the building, they could hear the janitor playing some pretty decent boogie-woogie on the piano.

"Listen to that," Carlton said.

"Yeah."

"Maybe we should have stayed longer," Carlton said, and laughed his nervous laugh. "For the encore." The lecture canceled, they suddenly had an entire evening to fill. What to do with so much surplus? Not enough time to catch a movie, yet too much time to kill before Katherine would need to head home, to her parents, to the questions she would invariably answer with lies. How was the lecture? Did you have a nice time?

"Yeah," Katherine said. "Maybe."

They crossed the campus quad, where frat boys played basketball late into the night, shirts versus skins, something Katherine could never believe, the way they shouted at the top of their lungs, oblivious to the dormitories around them. It began to feel cool outside; the temperature had dropped. Why could she never remember to bring a jacket when she needed it most?

"I guess we could just go back to your dorm," Katherine said.

Carlton said, "He was really good."

"The janitor?"

"Yeah."

Carlton watched the basketball game without quite paying attention, Katherine could tell. A shirtless player made an ill-advised pass, shouted an obscenity when a shirted player picked it off for an easy layup.

"I love it when things like that happen," Carlton said. "You know? When a working-class person does something society wouldn't expect."

"Oh."

"Like an air-conditioner repairman who also plays the cello," Carlton said, "or a construction worker who reads Proust."

"That doesn't seem like a quality you'd necessarily want in a construction worker," Katherine said. "Proust-certified."

Carlton gave her the look he sometimes gave her when she'd said something she'd later regret, something she thought she meant at the time but, after an excruciating review, which often included talking to herself in her car while tearfully chewing a Twix bar into semi-consoling globs, revealed itself to be something she should probably apologize for the next time she talked to him.

"I'm just saying it's a possibility," Carlton said.

Katherine often wondered if she should break up with Carlton. Should she? Hadn't she planned on breaking up with him several times, even to the point of wording her breakup in advance and practicing aloud in the shower? Didn't she think about breaking up with him nearly every time they were together? And even more often when they were apart? Why was she dating him at all, really?

To these questions, which daily assailed Katherine and at night crept into her dreams, she had arrived at a kind of answer, which was: she didn't know. Or at least she didn't think she knew. She didn't know if she should break up with Carlton. She didn't want to, necessarily, no matter how appealing the idea seemed sometimes. The thing was, she didn't have much to compare Carlton to, boyfriend-wise. She hadn't dated anyone before, aside from two movie dates with a boy from summer camp, Miles, who clasped Katherine's reluctant hand all through *The Return of the King* and later sent her creepy notes composed of letters scissored from *Sports Illustrated*. Her only other "boyfriend" had been a two-week relationship in eighth grade with a solemn boy named Juan who wordlessly escorted her to homeroom and wind ensemble, and later moved away with no explanation whatsoever. Juan! Where was he now? All she had to remember him by was a green penny he once removed from the trim of his Docksiders and handed to her with the gravitas of engagement ring.

Katherine and Carlton had started dating the spring before Carlton graduated high school. But they'd kept their relationship a secret, hidden. They both admitted to one another that they'd always been too nervous to date anyone in high school. Neither of them wanted to endure the burden of being a high school couple, the heat of public display, the daily pressure to strike the right pose, the school's collective censure burning upon them. No. They wouldn't deal with all of that. Instead, they'd be smart, Carlton assured her. They'd wait until summer and let summer shield them from view.

And that's exactly what they did. They went to movies, dinner, and readings. They played *Pictionary* and *Trivial Pursuit* with Katherine's parents, who warmed to Carlton, even if Katherine lately sensed her mother's disapproval, Katherine's visits to Carlton's dorm a new source of quiet unease between them. But the summer had passed smoothly, wonderfully even. Carlton was a dutiful boyfriend, respectful of curfews and family visits (Carlton had accompanied her to a family reunion in Maryland, where he'd charmed her younger cousins with card tricks) and was always eager to talk about college, with its promise of escape, its invitation to a life of the mind, to the project of thinking, to everything Carlton felt high school could only weakly recommend, high school too dense with football and peer pressure and marching band to give enlightenment a space big enough to roam.

Katherine liked Carlton's idealism, even if the idea of moving away to college next year terrified her, something she still wasn't quite able to think about. She would let Carlton be her forward scout, she decided. Yes. She'd get a taste of college, a preview of what it was like, glimpsed from the corner of her high school eye. She tried to see college the way Carlton did, even though she couldn't—not yet, at least. Still, she liked Carlton's enthusiasm. Unlike most of the guys she knew, Carlton wasn't afraid to show enthusiasm, even for things as hopelessly uncool as classical music. Over the summer he'd made her dozens of classical CDs. She'd listened to most of them, trying to hear what Carlton heard in the music. She liked some of them, but most of the music bored her. She'd end up putting on the radio or a CD of her own. Katherine needed music to be *songs*, and for those songs to have lyrics, or else she felt lonely, although she couldn't quite admit that to Carlton, who wouldn't understand.

What *did* Carlton understand about her? Probably not that much, Katherine thought. His second week of college, Carlton had loaned her a book they were reading in his creative writing class. A paperback whose gloomy cover showed a gloomy man staring gloomily into a television from which a cathedral gloomily glowed.

"I give you," Carlton had said, placing the book in her hands, "the greatest short story collection ever written by a human being." So far she had only read the first few pages of the first story, about a dumb guy who didn't want to go to another dumb guy's house for dinner. That didn't seem like much of a story to her, but maybe it got better later on. Maybe later on there would be some symbols and deep meanings. Like in *Brave New World* or *1984*. You couldn't read two sentences in *1984* without something deep and symbolic happening.

They left the basketball courts and walked along College Avenue, the main campus thoroughfare. It was starting to get dark out; Katherine would need to drive home soon, like always. At this time of night, the campus never failed to make her feel that she was getting away with something, passing as a college student, perhaps, she and Carlton locked arm in arm, something they almost never did in daylight, Katherine noted with some unease. Students passed in varying degrees of drunkenness and remarkably similar degrees of sweatshirts. Say what you want about college, Katherine thought, you couldn't fault its lack of merchandise. They stopped in front of a bookstore, closed now, whose window display showed the college's mascot reading a cookbook while roasting the rival school's mascot over a papier-mâché fire. *Get Cookin' for Homecoming!* a banner read, strung across the window.

"This is such a mediocre bookstore," Carlton said. He told her how he planned to take a road trip to Philadelphia to visit real bookstores as soon as his studies let up. Bookstores that had aisles and aisles of poetry and fiction, long as a department store's, and that contained the complete works of Tobias Wolff. Even *The Barracks Thief*, a masterpiece Carlton's creative writing professor had recommended to the entire class, despite its being more of a long short story than a novella in the proper sense.

They went to the newsstand instead, Carlton's choice, where Carlton crouched to his knees and gathered a stack of literary magazines, several of them as thick as books. "Here's the cream of the crop," he said, and held one up for Katherine to see.

"*The Paris Review.* Sounds nice."

Carlton handed it to her so that she might better remember where she was when she first heard the name of the magazine that was going to publish his first short story.

"They're going to publish a story of yours? That's incredible! How could you not tell me?"

Carlton pursed his lips into a wry smile. "Well, I believe I just did."

Katherine flipped through the magazine. "Is it in here?"

Carlton laughed. He took the pipe he'd started keeping in his cardigan pocket from the pocket and inserted it between his lips. The pipe was empty. "No, I haven't sent it to them yet."

"But I thought you said—"

"I said *The Paris Review* will be the magazine that *will* publish my first short story," Carlton said. "I have selected them to do so." He chewed thoughtfully on the pipe stem, which was riddled with teeth marks. "It is a commitment I've made. To myself. And to excellence itself."

"But when will you send it to them?"

"Only when it is finished," Carlton said.

Katherine flipped through the magazine. "When will you know when it's finished?"

Carlton said, "I will know in time." He took the pipe from his lips. "Only in time."

Later, they toured the sales racks outside the Five and Ten, more university sweatshirts upon more university sweatshirts. Katherine was going to say something about college making her never want to wear a sweatshirt again, but she wasn't sure how Carlton would take it. Lately it was getting harder and harder to figure him out. College had sort of done a number on him, she thought. He seemed to have acquired so many deeply held beliefs in such a short amount of time that they all crowded one another out, jostling for space in Carlton's rapidly expanding notion of himself. His opinions emerged as a rich composite of insight, speculation, and flat misunderstanding. His assertions arrived as firm and flimsy as newly dried glue.

When they passed the new pharmacy at the corner of Main Street and College Avenue, Carlton made a joke about everyone calling it the Condom Stop, the place where students stumbled after the bars were closing to stock up on condoms and munchies before staggering home to hook up with whomever, the way everybody did. Katherine made a joke that maybe they should stop by and get some, too. Carlton turned to look at her.

"Are you serious?"

Katherine nodded.

Carlton got the concerned look he sometimes got whenever she grabbed the wheel and started steering the conversation to places he hadn't expected. "Do you think you really are, though? Serious?"

Katherine thought she was. "I think I am," she said.

"Because that's what I'm asking you. Whether you're serious or not."

"I know. I mean, I am. Serious."

Carlton reminded her that this was a subject they'd broached before. Katherine responded yes, she knew that. Carlton said he wanted to point out that he had not forced this conversation. Katherine agreed that he had not forced this conversation. And certainly she knew, he said, that this decision was one that would have repercussions for their relationship and would produce emotions—ones that would likely include disappointment, if they were being honest—and might complicate their relationship, wouldn't she agree? Katherine said he had a point. Well, then, Carlton wanted to know, was it worth the risk? Katherine said that nearly everything was a risk when you thought about it. True, Carlton said, but had she really thought about it?

Katherine thought about it. "I think I kind of just want to get it over with," she said.

It was crowded inside the pharmacy. A line of students snaked from the register to the front doors. Carlton and Katherine pushed through the line, a sudden whiff of new carpet and beery sweat. Katherine took the long way to the Family Needs aisle, surprised by how easy it was to find. Usually she couldn't find anything when she went inside a pharmacy. Especially deodorant, which her mom usually picked up for her anyway, but still, that would change soon; she would have to buy her own deodorant next year, a thought that struck her with a strange and embarrassing poignancy. Katherine turned to tell Carlton what she was thinking but found that he had disappeared. She backtracked to the magazine aisle, where she could distinctly recall Carlton glancing at the shelves, but the only person standing there now was a woman in a cape reading *InStyle* magazine. The woman's cape seemed to be made of felt, or wool, or possibly both, Katherine couldn't tell. Were those the same things? The woman was reading aloud, but not loud enough that Katherine could make out the words.

But where was Carlton? Katherine looked in all the places she had already looked. She knew it was ridiculous, but she couldn't think of anything else to do. People gave her looks as she passed them by again, or so it seemed. The cashier asked if she needed help with anything. She shook her head no. A few moments later, she pushed through the front door and found Carlton standing outside beside a bike rack. He was chewing his pipe and inspecting the bikes like he was trying to remember which one was his. When she approached, Carlton gave her the smile he sometimes gave her when he was about to say something maddening. "So," he whispered, "did you get them?"

"What?"

"The, well, you know," Carlton said. He glanced behind him, over one shoulder, then the other. "The things."

"The *things*?"

"I saw you heading toward them."

"Why did you leave me in there? I thought you were right behind me."

"I was," Carlton said. "But then I thought it might be better for you to get them."

"Why would you think that?"

"You seemed to know where they were," Carlton said, "and I felt a little uncomfortable, seeing as how I might bump into someone I know." Carlton inspected the wide handlebars of a cruiser bike. The handlebars had pom-poms exploding from their ends. "I thought it was better for me to head outside. You know, far from prying eyes."

"You left me in there because you were scared you might see someone you know?"

"Well," Carlton said, "it is a potential risk."

"You asshole."

"I don't know why you have to use that language. I never use bad words when speaking to you."

"Are you serious? I'm speaking to you that way because you ran away and left me alone in a store to buy condoms for you so that we could have sex for the first time."

"Well," Carlton said, "when you put it that way, it sounds terrible."

"That's because it *is* terrible. It's really, really terrible."

Carlton hung his head, a scolded child. After a moment, he said, "I'm sorry. I just wanted to avoid running into anyone I know because I wanted to protect your privacy. That's all. I didn't want to give you away." Carlton gave her a hopeful smile. "I was only thinking of you."

"Oh, Jesus," Katherine sighed. "Just give me some money."

Katherine bought the condoms, pricier than she imagined, not drawing attention from anyone, not even the cape woman, who got the register next to hers and bought, in addition to the *InStyle* magazine, an entire basket full of travel-sized Excedrin. Outside it was dark. Katherine would need to be getting home soon. She hated the way she was always thinking about what time it was whenever she was with Carlton, the meter forever running. That was another thing she would never tell Carlton—that and the fact that she knew she was going to cry later thinking about the cape woman buying all that Excedrin.

Carlton's room: two twin beds keeping a minifridge company. A lone window wearing curtains the approximate color and thickness of sandwich bread. Two desks hilariously fitted out with goose-necked lamps, in the unlikely event of studying. The room felt cold, although it was only September, still warm in the daytime, occasionally hot. For no reason whatsoever Katherine recalled that she had a book report on *Brave New World* due the following Monday. She'd already read it the summer before, so no big deal, but still, good thing she remembered. She didn't want to slack her senior year away the way so many of her friends were. Sometimes she felt so much older than them it was insane, even though feeling superior to people was something she was totally not into.

"Let's lie down," she whispered.

Carlton gave her his deepest, eyes-closed kiss, which gave her a moment to study his face up close, something she liked to do from time to time. At this distance his expression seemed to convey both his deep feeling and total indifference for her. *It's all about him*, she thought, not for the first time. Maybe she still had that paper she'd written about *Brave New World* from last year. But there was no way she could use that paper again. She'd get caught for sure.

They sat down on the bed.

"We really don't have to," Carlton whispered.

"I know."

"Please don't feel like we have to," Carlton said, although he'd already nearly broken Katherine's bra clasp, trying to do it the wrong way like he always did.

"Let's get underneath the covers," Katherine said. "I'm freezing."

"Okay." But when they pulled the covers off, Carlton remembered that he'd stripped the bed earlier that day: the mattress, a flabby and homely thing, stared back at them. "I could put the old sheets on," Carlton offered. "Or something?"

"Do you have an extra blanket?"

Carlton considered this. "Not personally."

Katherine had no idea why Carlton never had extra linens. Her mom kept about ten different sets in their hallway closet, folded into neat squares. That was one thing Katherine had learned about college: no one had extra linens. Goodbye, the abundance of home. Farewell surplus, hello stark mattress faintly patterned with roses. "I'm not getting on that mattress," she said.

"Hold on," Carlton said. He sprang from the bed and opened his bottom dresser drawer. "We could use these." He held up two long-sleeved Polo shirts Katherine couldn't ever recall him wearing.

"Where'd you get those?"

"Eddie gave them to me when we first moved in," Carlton admitted. Eddie was Carlton's roommate. "His mom sends them to him."

"Those won't work."

"I can't believe this."

"We could just use the cover as a blanket," Katherine said. "Sort of like a sleeping bag."

"We could."

"Let's try," Katherine said.

The blanket was just large enough to wrap around them, but not large enough to cover Carlton's backside whenever Katherine moved, which she had to do often, to keep Carlton's arm from hurting her. "Could you move your arm out from under me?" Katherine said. "It's kind of in the way." The blanket brought Carlton's face closer than their other sessions usually did, and Katherine was alarmed to see that his expression, usually exuding grateful expectation by this point, couldn't find its traditional purchase. Instead, he stared at her as if she'd handed him a pop final exam.

"Ouch," Katherine said, "you're on my hair."

"Sorry."

Katherine could feel Carlton's erection against her legs, which still hadn't been shorn of their underwear, a task complicated by the blanket, which made spreading her legs apart nearly impossible, and was going to make everything that was to follow nearly impossible as well. "I don't think this is going to work," Katherine said.

"I wasn't forcing you!" Carlton said. "I always said we didn't have to do this."

"Oh, would you please shut up? I only mean this blanket isn't going to work, that's all." She told him to get the cleanest sheet he could find from his laundry basket and bring it to the bed. Carlton complied, but not before pausing at his stereo. "Purcell or Mahler?" he asked.

"No music."

"Are you sure? I always find Purcell to be helpful at times like these."

"Carlton," Katherine said, "I'm cold and naked and only have twenty minutes before I have to leave and you are driving me crazy, so would you please not say anything for a while and get back over here before I change my mind?"

Carlton said, "Which you can, if you want."

But Katherine didn't. She pulled the laundry sheet around them. Carlton struggled to put the condom on, saying sorry every three seconds. He tried again, narrating why it was hard to tell which part was the top of the condom and which part was the bottom.

"You're really killing the mood," Katherine said.

"I'm only trying to be honest."

"Be less honest then."

"Less honest?"

"Less honest, more faster," Katherine said.

"I don't think that's good advice."

"Just hurry up, okay?"

Carlton hurried up, completed his task, then turned to kiss her. Katherine kissed him back and realized, with a surprise that shouldn't have been all that surprising, that she was going to have to be the one to direct him after all. Of course she would, Carlton's kisses told her. She would be the one to carry them across the threshold of regret and awkwardness, no looking back.

"Okay," she said.

Carlton looked at her. "We both know this is going to be disappointing," he said.

Katherine sighed. "Just get on top of me."

Carlton moved on top of her. His face, from this slightly new angle, revealed a chicken pox scar clinging to the underside of his left nostril. "I feel like my entire life has been preparing me for the ecstasy and disappointment of this moment," he mused. He was looking to the window, although the curtains were drawn.

"I know what you mean," Katherine said. "It's like everything tells you how disappointing it's going to be."

"Everything," Carlton said. He was barely moving inside her, cautious, unsure.

"Everything," Katherine agreed. She opened her eyes for a moment, which only served to inform her that she had closed them at all. How strange Carlton looked, she thought. How odd. And people said this act was natural? Katherine had some words for those people, she did. She tried to think about her book report. Was the report due Monday or not? This question the only thought she had. She could feel it inside her, lonely thought, wandering around until another arrived: maybe the report was on *1984* instead of *Brave New World*? She was always getting those two mixed up somehow.

After they'd finished, after Carlton had apologized for the umpteenth time about his performance, and after Katherine had returned from the dormitory bathroom and sat back down on Carlton's bed, Katherine was surprised to discover that she'd begun to cry.

"What's wrong?" Carlton said. "Did I hurt you?"

"No."

"You're crying."

"It's nothing."

"What's the matter?" Carlton said. He put his arm around her.

"I'm just feeling sad."

"Was it something I did?" Carlton said.

"No."

"It would kill me if I knew it was something I did."

Katherine shook her head, wiped her eyes. "Sometimes I just get really sad," she said, which was true. She usually cried at least once every day, although she would never reveal that to Carlton. The night before she'd cried while watching a TV movie with her mom. The movie was about a train carrying orphans to the prairie where, after a series of hardships, each orphan found a perfect home. *A Perfect Home*, it was called.

"I'm sorry if I did something to make you cry," Carlton whispered. "I really am." He tried to kiss her, but Katherine turned away.

"I think it was this woman," Katherine said.

"A woman?"

"This woman at the store tonight." She began to sob. "She was buying so much Excedrin."

"Oh."

"She had a cape."

Carlton drew her closer, so that her face burned wetly against his shoulder, and said, "I know what you mean." But he didn't, Katherine knew; he didn't understand her at all.

After an awkward and soul-crushing round of gathering her things together while not saying anything, Katherine left Carlton's dorm. She made her way across the quad. It was late enough that she would need to hurry, but not late enough that she couldn't stop by the basketball courts and watch the frat boys play shirts versus skins, just for a few moments, she told herself, while she prepared a few lies for home. The shirts were running up and down the court on the skins, their passes taut and clean. The skins took weak defensive positions, missed easy takeaways, threw two passes out of bounds on two consecutive possessions. When the skins finally blocked a shot from the perimeter, they missed a layup on the other end. Katherine put her hands to the fence, worked her fingers through. "Come on!" she said, replaying her father's words, on those Saturday mornings when she'd played junior varsity ball, the gymnasium fitted out with sleepy parents taking long sips from Styrofoam cups, their eyes barely following the game.

"Offense," she said, "don't let your eyes tell them your pass!"

Those mornings, Katherine had felt the basketball's pleasant weight against her fingers, its stippled skin a strange cantaloupe submitting to her will. Her feet made kissing noises on the gymnasium floor. Her next shot arranged itself before her, the way it sometimes did.

"Defense," she said. "Get back or get had!"

She'd been good at tuning her father out while tuning him in, too, a dutiful daughter with superior footwork. She'd been good at getting the better of things back then. The ball had usually given her a favorable bounce and roll.

"Watch the weak side!" she said.

Except that she wasn't saying it, these frat boys' expressions would have her know; she was shouting it. Pounding her fists against the fence. Her face was raw from crying. Her expression impossible to read. Who was this girl, out late at night, on her way to wherever, wanting them to do so many things? They turned their faces toward her, their breath catching in their chests, eager for instruction.

Hey, Me

'm checking to see if this works. Hey, this is me, checking to see if this works. Hello? Okay, I just checked and this works. I'm back, even though you didn't know I was gone. Ha, I say to you. Foolish you. So easily tricked by my mastery of technology.

I feel like I should say who I am and why I'm making this recording, but I think I'm the only person who will ever listen to it, unless I really do get up the nerve to send it to you, Professor. Other than that happening, though, I guess there's no point. Except to say, hey, it's me, your one and only me, doing what you already know I'm doing and why. Today is Sunday. Weather: cloudy. Barometer: steady. Winds out of the direction they are out of.

I'm standing in front of my stove, which I hardly ever use. The stove is a Kenmore. Something I never noticed until now. What else? Electric. Black with black dials. Four heating elements, but only two of them work. The stove has a hood or an overhang, or whatever you call those things that have a fan and a light. The light is my favorite part of the stove. It's got a really satisfying click when you hit the switch. There, ah! Did you hear that? I just turned it on. The light is soft and pretty much useless, but I like it anyway. At night, if you turn off all of the other lights and sit at the kitchen table with the stove light on, you can almost get this churchy sort of feeling.

If this recording achieves nothing else, it will help me come to terms with my deep, complex, and conflicted feelings about my home furnishings.

Speaking of which, big news: I'm opening one of the kitchen drawers now. This drawer has so much junk in it. Hear that? A real treasure trove. Let's see. We have one Chinese menu, authentically wrinkled and sauce stained. One pack of Post-it notes—pink, not yellow. A magnetized bottle opener that used to be on my refrigerator until the magnet stopped working for some mysterious reason. Coupons for Starbucks Pike Place Medium Roast coffee, expired over five months ago. The engagement ring my ex-fiancé Ian once gave me. Paperclips, both large and small, but mostly the small kind.

But I digress from my digression. Now *that's* digressive, she said, having no idea what she meant by that.

Okay, no more kitchen tours. No more insecurity masked as self-awareness.

Let me cut to the chase.

As they say.

One time I followed you on campus, Professor. I want to apologize for doing that. I'm sorry. I realize how creepy it sounds, mostly because it is creepy, plus stalky, plus embarrassing. I didn't mean to. Not exactly. What happened was I went to your office, but you didn't answer when I knocked on your door, so I stood there for a minute, like an idiot, thinking that maybe you had changed your office hours, and then I decided to go down to the office and ask the admin if she knew what your office hours were this semester, but when I started walking downstairs, I heard you talking to the admin and I just stopped on the stairs and listened. I could hear you talking to the admin, and you were sort of joking around with her, and she was laughing at whatever you were saying, which kind of surprised me, since you aren't the kind of professor who jokes around much, I mean, as a professor, when you are in your full-on professor persona. By which I don't mean to say that your teaching persona is an act; I only mean to say that I understand that we all act in different ways in different social contexts, and that acting different ways in different contexts doesn't mean that someone is superficial or two-faced or shallow or whatever. Honestly, I've never totally gotten the strike against being two-faced. I can't imagine what a one-faced person would be like. Plus I really like that you aren't a jokey professor. The world needs fewer of those, in my opinion.

Anyhow: the stairway. I stood in the stairway and listened to you talk with the admin, and then you must have said goodbye and walked outside because I couldn't hear anyone talking anymore, so I went down the stairs, and there you weren't, so to speak, so I walked outside, too, and saw you walking along the pedestrian mall. You were wearing your shoulder bag, plus you had a heavy-looking canvas tote bag in your other hand that must have had books or student papers in it, or maybe that's where you keep your laptop?

I started walking behind you for no real reason except that I had this movie playing in my head where I would catch up to you and say, "Hey, Professor, do you need some help carrying those?" even though I knew you would say no, but at the same time, I felt like you would have a favorable impression of me for offering, and you would get in your car later and think, "Amy reminds me of me back when I was in college. Yes, I certainly see a lot of myself in her." And that idea just made me super happy. So I kept following you, although you could just say I was walking a few feet behind you on the pedestrian mall, since that's all it would look like to anyone watching.

The whole time I followed you, I kept getting this feeling that you knew I was there. Like you could sense it, maybe, and that you were about to turn around and say, "I thought that was you," and then I would explain about knocking on your office door and you would say, "Why don't we sit here for a moment and talk?" and then we'd sit together on one of those uncomfortable donor benches they've got all along the pedestrian mall and talk, and I'd give all my usual evasive answers about why I was struggling to complete my papers, and you would nod thoughtfully and smile, and the whole time you'd be thinking how I reminded you of you back in college, and you'd be wondering whether you should say something like that to me, and then you would decide no, that wouldn't be a good thought to share, too intimate, too personal, too much crossing a boundary, even though I would know you only decided that out of teacher/student propriety, when really you wanted to tell me all about your undergraduate self, and somehow you would know that I knew that, and smile, and it would be like we were incredible friends sitting on a bench in the middle of campus.

You crossed the quad and passed in front of the memorial union. I followed. Outside the memorial union, student groups were hosting bake sales, fundraising drives. An honor society hawked T-shirts and coffee mugs. A sorority was selling Rice Krispies squares wrapped in pink cellophane. One of the sorority students called out to you and waved. Hey, Professor! Want to buy a Rice Krispies treat? You stopped to say hello and chat with her. I could see you nodding at whatever she was saying. The student kept talking. She must have been telling you some funny story; you nodded politely, laughed appropriately. She offered you a Rice Krispies treat, possibly on the house, but you put up your hands as if to say, Not for me, sorry, but thanks. The student made a face that seemed to ask, Are you sure? And you raised your hands again, as if to say, I'm sure. All right, the student said—I could read this even from where I stood, thirty feet or so away, feigning interest in a poster sale, embarrassingly bad stuff, heavy on stoner films—and then you said goodbye, waved, and continued on your way. You put your canvas tote bag across your shoulder. You picked up your pace.

I went up to the sorority table and bought the Rice Krispies treat. The same one the student had offered you. One dollar. I guess my plan was to follow you and then give you the Rice Krispies treat, or maybe I would somehow use the Rice Krispies treat as an icebreaker of sorts, kind of like a prop, as in, Oh, hey professor, funny to see you out here walking past the memorial union at the same time as me. Do you want some of this Rice Krispies treat? Are you sure? I can't finish the whole thing, etc., etc. I had this scene in my head where I was offering you the Rice Krispies treat and you were saying no, and then you eventually agreed to split it with me, and we stood together outside the memorial union eating our Rice Krispies treat, feeling this tremendous unspoken understanding between us.

"A lot of the time," I imagined myself saying, "I feel anxious around people. Like, nearly all the time."

"Me, too," you said.

"Really?" I said.

"You have no idea," you said. And then you told me all about it. How nervous you got before teaching. How you dreaded having to enter the classroom. How you had to steel yourself before every student conference. How you knew your colleagues found you awkward and aloof. How sometimes you felt like you were using your new baby as a shield against personal interactions with colleagues and students, where, by adopting the role of mother and parent, instead of teacher or department member, you could slip between the seams of your social unease, even though doing that and being aware of doing that made you feel horrible. Like, not only were you a social strikeout but a bad mother, too.

"I'm sure you're not a bad mother," I imagined saying. You shrugged, said, "Only time will tell, I guess."

And then I saw us sitting there, just really getting into hanging out with each other, not having to say a word, our fingers sticky with sugar. We sat that way for a while, not saying anything, in my childish-stupid imagined scene. But I let it play in my head for a while, and then I realized I'd lost sight of you. I walked a little faster, and I guess I must have pushed past some slow-walking students, because what happened next was that I pushed through another group of students and then another, and that's when I saw you sitting on a bench at the very end of the pedestrian mall. You had your bags at your feet and were sitting with your legs crossed. You had your phone to your ear. You were smiling, laughing at what the other person was saying. You sat that way for a while. Then you put your phone away and reached into your canvas tote bag.

And pulled out a Rice Krispies treat. Still wrapped in pink cellophane.

I watched as you unwrapped the cellophane (I was standing behind some bushes at this point, pretending to check my phone) and took your first bite. You chewed the treat and then wiped your lips what seemed too many times. Then you broke a piece off with your hands, instead, and then tucked it into your mouth when no one was passing by. I got the feeling that you were slightly embarrassed to be seen eating in public. Something I totally understand, by the way, since I'm the same way too. I hate eating in public. The way my mouth looks when I'm chewing. Makes me feel like I'm on display.

I watched you until you rewrapped the remainder of the Rice Krispies treat, placed it into your canvas bag, and stood from the bench. You straightened your skirt, checked your phone once again. Then you placed the bag across your shoulder and headed off to the faculty parking lot, I'm guessing, since that seemed like where you were headed.

I walked back across the pedestrian mall the same way as I had come. I passed the memorial union and the sorority girls selling baked goods. I passed the poster sale and all the rest. I tossed the Rice Krispies treat into a trash can. The trash can had three holes, each one for a different kind of recycling. Those trash cans always make me feel guilty about something, I don't even know what.

So you had accepted the Rice Krispies treat all along. Maybe you had placed it in your bag when I was looking at the posters. Maybe you had it in your hand and then slipped it into the bag when I was following you down the pedestrian mall. I don't know. I guess it really doesn't matter. I walked along the pedestrian mall and tried to turn the whole thing into a story, but I couldn't decide what kind of story it was. I imagined telling you about it the next day, a funny little anecdote about me buying you a Rice Krispies treat and then seeing you eat your own Rice Krispies treat, but I couldn't imagine it as a funny little anecdote somehow, and my imagination wouldn't budge. My imagination was like, I have no idea, Amy.

Jesus, I can't even tell this right. I wanted to talk about the time I followed you around campus and saw you eating a Rice Krispies treat and how that experience helped me understand something about you and about teachers and students but also about college too. Because it was all so clear to me when I first started talking about it, and then suddenly it wasn't. Suddenly it was this semipathetic story about me following you around like a puppy dog and then having my puppy-dog heart broken by watching you eat a one-dollar bake sale treat.

Let me try again.

Insert throat clearing.

Add nervous stammering.

The day I followed you around made me realize there was this other side to you. This side I didn't know. I mean, I understand that being a professor or a teacher means adopting a persona or an identity that's different from the one you use in the rest of your life (it would be weird if you didn't change out of your professor identity, actually), but when I followed you around that day, it was like I saw how happy you were to escape that persona, at least for a few moments, the way you chatted so easily with your student outside of the classroom, with nothing at stake beyond whether to accept a free baked good or not. You seemed at ease, in a way I'd never seen you at ease before. Like you were a different person altogether. And it made me wonder what your life must be like beyond the classroom and if, whenever you entered that other part of your life, you felt like you could truly be yourself, or at least closer to your true self, whatever that is, without having to care about how you came across to others.

And then that got me thinking about all of my other professors. And then thinking about all my other professors got me thinking about all of college. And then thinking about all of college got me thinking about all of the incompletes I had to finish. And I know this sounds self-serving and disingenuous, because it really is, but I just got this sudden feeling that college was a kind of persona too, or maybe a shared persona, if that makes sense.

No, it does not make sense.

Try again, Amy.

What I felt was that college was a kind of show we were all putting on together. An act. Not that it was a bad act, necessarily; in fact, it's kind of a beautiful act, in certain ways, in ways that are kind of important to me, actually, but still an act nonetheless. And I began to see that maintaining the act was sort of agreed upon by everyone, in the same way that we agreed on going to class twice a week and sitting in a semicircle in the homey glow of your PowerPoint presentation while munching on salty snacks and secretly IM-ing about your fashion choices.

See what I mean?

Me neither.

But maybe I mean that we all somehow participated in the act. We sat in class and felt the act embrace us, as real and substantial as the silence that attended nearly every class discussion. That inescapable and soul-sucking silence broken only by the same two or three students who participated each and every class, almost on cue, almost as if the act depended upon it. We wanted those two or three students to raise their familiar observations, nearly indistinguishable from their last observations and the observations before those, and keep the act aloft. That was something we needed. That was something important.

This is all coming out wrong.

Treat all of this with the highest possible degree of skepticism.

This isn't what I really mean.

None of this is what I really mean.

What I really mean is one time I stopped inside the student center to buy a bottle of water before class. The student center dining hall was completely empty except for one table fitted out with a dozen freshmen—from the same dorm, I'm guessing—all huddled together over their dining hall trays. They were eating soggy chicken sandwiches and waffle fries. They joked and laughed about whatever. Someone said, "Make Andrew stop saying that!" and then someone said, "Andrew said it was true!" and then someone threw a waffle fry at someone who must have been Andrew, and Andrew ate it. Everyone laughed. Everyone joked nervously. They said things that probably weren't funny at all, things that they maybe wouldn't have laughed at in any other situation, but here they laughed at them like they were the funniest things they'd ever heard.

Outside it was dark. I could see the students' reflection in the dining hall windows. They were seated so close together. And it occurred to me that the students weren't actually having fun. The students were actually scared. Scared to be out at night, so far from home, so invested in new friendships that maybe weren't even friendships at all yet and never would be. So unsure of what pose to strike, what person to be, what attitude to adopt. All of that was still up for grabs. The only thing to do now was huddle together and laugh and joke until the laughter and joking felt genuine. Until the friendships took hold. What else could they do?

I don't know what I'm saying.

I don't get it either.

I don't know what the dining hall students have to do with anything, except that as I watched them, I felt this intense kind of longing for something genuine and sincere, even though I *hate* using those words, ugh, and I hate positioning myself as some kind of seeker of all that is true and real. What I mean is that I suddenly felt that I didn't want to do anything that was insincere anymore. I only wanted to do things that felt honest, even though honest isn't the right word. But I felt it: only sincere actions from now on.

And somehow that included my incomplete paper, since I didn't know how to make it sincere, since I never believed a word I was saying whenever I tried to write it. I'd start off with some terrible opening, meant to sound like I knew what I was talking about, until I could hit the reader with my thesis statement, and then I could see all of the moves ahead of me: making everything fit, making everything support my argument, one insincere paragraph yielding to the next until I reached the end, clapped my hands together, and said, Well, let's hope no one notices I didn't mean any of that. And I just couldn't do it anymore. I couldn't write the paper.

But I could keep the paper as is, incomplete, since the incomplete paper was more sincere than the completed paper would ever be. At least the incomplete had that going for it. You couldn't fault those blank pages for a lack of sincerity.

So that's sort of what happened.

I think.

Or maybe it's not what happened.

Okay, I'm going to save this until I have the courage to delete it. This is what passes for bravery in Amy's world.

Hey, it's me. I'm back.

Hey, me.

Hey, that kind of sounds like my name.

Hey-me.

Amy.

Hmm. Compare/contrast. Draw conclusions. Discuss.

So it's been one day since I recorded my last memo, and I'm proud to say I haven't listened to it once. But what's even better is that I've started this new voice memo without erasing the last one. Is there no end to Amy's achievements? No, there is not. Amy's achievements amaze and inspire us all.

Okay, I will knock it off with the third person. It's kind of sad that I'm most comfortable talking about myself in the third person. Insert philosophical reflection about the reasons and motivations behind one thinking of oneself in a non–first-person perspective. I'm already imagining the two of us talking philosophical-like, Professor, except that we aren't hanging out at your office or even at my crappy apartment, the way I sometimes imagine. No, not this time. This time we're just in a sort of philosophical non-space, some intermittent landscape. Sort of like Charlie Brown and Linus standing behind a low wall, talking about life, depression, and the hollowness of secular observances of religious holidays. Can you picture that? A few tufts of grass penciled in here and there. Maybe a fat cloud or two in the sky above, to give a suggestion of real life. Whatever that is, right?

Anyway, the main thing is that I'm back to first person, and the second main thing is that I am going to answer your burning question: Did I really say I had an ex-fiancé?

I did.

And did I really say his name was Ian?

Yes. Was and is.

And did I really say that his engagement ring was still in my kitchen drawer?

Yes again.

And wouldn't I have to admit that mentioning my ex-fiancé and my ex-fiancé's engagement ring in passing, with no greater emphasis than mentioning, say, that I was about to toast a slice of bread, is a telling sign in itself, one that likely bears upon my incomplete papers and might be the very key to unlocking this peculiar little mystery as to why I'm standing in my kitchen yet again, recording a voice memo to you, my suddenly curious professor, who now feels she's about this close to solving The Case of Amy's Incomplete Paper? (I was holding my fingers an inch apart when I said "about this close.")

Well?

Well, I'm so glad you mentioned toast. The truth is, I can't get enough of the stuff. I have something like a bad toast habit, I really do. It goes like this: I'll be sitting in my apartment, idle me idly doing not much of anything (especially not writing term papers, ha, ha, hardy-har-har), when this thought just sort of settles upon me that maybe I could escape my current situation by making a slice of toast. So off to the kitchen I go. I remove a loaf of bread from the freezer (I freeze my bread, one of Ian's pet peeves, among many), unwrap it, and pry one slice of reluctant bread from the rest. Next, I drop the slice of bread into the toaster. My favorite part: watching the toaster coils heat up. The way they turn orange. You can see them doing that incrementally, but you have to be as committed to staring at a toaster heating up as I am.

Toast, it's just like everyone always says: it demands everything of you.

Have you noticed that I'm not beating myself up for telling jokes? Because I was just imagining this scene in my head where you were listening to this and thinking how proud you were that I was allowing myself to do that. For some reason you were wearing a hat, something I've never actually seen you wear. Insert probable meaning of imagined hat.

Something you don't absolutely need to know: during my toast speech, I wandered into the living room and checked the Weather Channel, which is something I sometimes do for no apparent reason. Why didn't you hear me do that, you ask? Aha, because I muted the TV.

The thing is, I was only using the toast speech to buy a little time to think about what I wanted to say about Ian. My first thought was to reveal this semi-embarrassing thing, and my next thought was maybe that wasn't the best option, but then this third thought came along and was like, Just go with the first thing.

So, okay, the first thing: Ian used to cover his ears whenever I used the bathroom.

I had no idea until this one time I was using the bathroom, or was about to use the bathroom, I guess I should say. Ian and I were in bed, reading on our laptops, when I got up to use the bathroom. I closed the bathroom the door behind me and lifted the toilet lid just before I noticed we were out of toilet paper. I guess I should mention that the toilet lid made a clunking sound when I'd lifted it. An important detail. Anyway, I knew we had some toilet paper in the hall closet, so I went to get some, and when I opened the bathroom door, I saw

Ian sitting on the bed with his laptop in front of him, his hands pressed to his ears. Firmly. Like a fire engine was passing by. He had his eyes closed, too, so he didn't see me standing there for a moment. His mouth was drawn into a line. He was humming to himself, quietly. I could hear him doing that. After a few seconds—when Ian didn't hear the toilet flush through his flattened ears, I'm guessing—he opened his eyes and saw me staring at him from the bathroom doorway. He quickly put his hands down.

"Do you always do that?" I asked.

"Do what?" he said.

"Cover your ears when I'm using the bathroom."

"Oh," he said. But he didn't elaborate. He just went back to his laptop like we weren't talking.

So I said, "Why do you do that?"

But Ian only shrugged.

"Because you don't want to hear anything," I said. "Obviously. Right?"

Ian typed something on his keypad, even though I knew he just wanted to give me the impression he was working on something, which he wasn't.

"Why do you close your eyes?" I asked.

Ian said, "I didn't realize I was doing that." But he wasn't even looking at me. He was still looking at his laptop.

I don't know why it's important to mention that Ian wasn't looking at me: why *would* Ian look at me? I wouldn't look at me either if I had just been caught covering my ears while my fiancée was using the bathroom. I guess I just wanted to give a picture of Ian sitting there in bed with his laptop. Which is actually a pretty honest picture of our entire relationship, the two of us in a room together, in separate spaces, staring into separate laptops. Sort of like an Edward Hopper painting. Except with laptops.

Hmm. I'm struggling to see the relevance of that memory.

Guess what thought just crossed my mind? Toast! Yes, it's time for toast. We will now take a short break while Amy makes toast.

You didn't think it could happen, but oh, then it happens: I'm back.

Hey, Amy, welcome back.

Hey, me.

Surprising revelation: it's been one day since I paused the recording. Tuesday, for all of those following closely. Yea, I say to you that the sun hath sinketh in the sky and arisen again in the interim of Amy's toasting of bread and the present dawn, which sendeth long shadows across her kitchenette. Who knew you could pause a voice memo for an entire day? If anything, this project has awakened my admiration for voice memos. Voice memos: they're more than just a squiggly-looking app you never use and have no feelings about whatsoever.

Oh, the jokes. They keep coming. What can one do?

Solution: we can talk about our last office meeting. Shall I set the stage, or is that stage all too familiar to you? Your office, door open, chair drawn to the front of your desk, which, based upon my visits to other professors' offices, you keep quite clean, spartan, almost. You've got some personal effects, as they say, arranged near the printer I've never seen you use, some academic-looking award thingy on a black pedestal, an espresso maker, plus a box of baby toys, including a brightly colored abacus.

And now let us introduce one Amy into this familiar scene, arriving five minutes late, her bookbag leaden with textbooks she has barely cracked and can hardly wait to sell back to the college bookstore the minute finals week is done rearing its frightening head. Here she is, taking the chair across from you and apologizing like a maniac for being late while you tell her no problem at all. You have your baby with you today, you say, so you know what it's like trying to keep to a schedule. The two of you turn your attention to the baby, who stares back at you, blankly, from a Pack 'n Play in a corner of the office. A boy or a girl, Amy can't remember, but definitely one or the other. Having introduced Amy into this dull tableau, and having established that she isn't exactly what you would call a baby person, I will now switch back to first person, since I was having trouble with the third person.

Or was that second person? Have I mentioned I'm an English major?

So: we exchanged pleasantries. I asked about the baby, and you answered, even though you aren't one of those professors who is always talking about their children. I imagined myself asking if that was by intention and imagined you laughing and saying it was. This scene played in my head where we made fun of professors who talk too much about their kids, and everything you said was incredibly witty and observant, and I was trying to match you, joke for joke. But really that didn't happen, of course. Really you just asked me how things were going. I said they were going, except for how they weren't. You nodded like that was exactly what you thought I was going to say.

"What seems to be the main problem?" you said.

I thought about it. "Well, me, mainly," I said.

You laughed. "Anything else?" you said.

I said, "I guess after me, I'd have to say everything else."

You gave me a look. I don't want to say this look was practiced looking, necessarily, but let's just say I could see it was a look you've probably mastered over the years. Wait, isn't that the same thing? Anyway, you gave me your look and said, "Writing is hard."

I said, "Yeah."

"So there's no need to make it any harder," you said. "The difficulty is already built in."

I said I knew you were right. Who could argue otherwise?

You gave me some suggestions. I nodded and said those were good suggestions, because they were good suggestions and because I felt like nodding. You said wise things. You said things meant to inspire me to action without criticizing me for my inaction. You struck the perfect balance between criticism and encouragement. You said things I knew were true and right and gleaned from the very stuff of your lived life.

You said, "Most writing problems aren't *writing* problems."

You said, "Most writing problems are *thinking* problems."

You said, "Don't try to outfox your paper."

You said, "Let your paper outfox *you*."

And I nodded and said right, right, and I knew you were genuinely helping me, and I knew you knew it too. Normally, that kind of thing would make me happy, but for some reason it didn't. Instead, this weird thing started happening where I felt myself getting disappointed by what you were saying, since what you were saying felt maybe not totally super sincere, or at least felt like something I could tell you've said a million times to students before. Which doesn't mean it wasn't useful, because I actually think it was, or most of it was, at least, but I couldn't help feeling disappointed, and I found myself nodding like an idiot because I didn't want you to know how disappointed I actually was. I listened to whatever you were saying next, but the whole time I was secretly imagining us talking about what I was feeling.

"I don't think that's entirely fair of you," imaginary you said, "to think that I'm being insincere because I'm saying things I've said to students before."

"I know," imaginary me said. "It isn't."

"Look, Amy," you said, but then I couldn't think of what imaginary you would say next, so it got imaginary awkward all of a sudden. We sat that way for a while. We felt time's passage. A nondog barked in the nondistance.

After a while imaginary me said, "I know what you want to say."

"That I could never live up to your notion of me," you said.

"Right," I said.

"Because no one could," you said.

"Right," I said.

"And even though that's something you understand intuitively and accept as truth," you said, "you still have a hard time accepting it."

"True," I said. "Like so many things!"

You smiled. Then you sat for a moment with your hand on your chin, in a poor approximation of someone lost deep in thought, my fault entirely.

"Listen," you said.

"You want to tell me that teachers sometimes loom larger in their students' lives than students loom in theirs," I offered.

"Yes," you said.

"And you want me to know, in a way that affirms your kind feelings for me without overstating them, too, that although you enjoy having me in class and enjoy meeting with me from time to time, you understand our relationship primarily as one between teacher and student. And nothing more," I said.

You said, "Yes."

"And now you want to explain to me that, even though it isn't possible for us to pursue a friendship at the present moment, you are not averse, and have not in fact been averse in the past, to keeping in touch with former students, either through email or social media or both, and can very well see the two of us following along that path," I said.

And here's the part where I want to say *you smiled warmly* or *you gave me an encouraging look*, but that's not what happened at all. What happened was your baby started crying. Big, huge crying that honestly sort of freaked me out. I didn't realize babies could cry so loud.

But your baby was wanting to help me understand new things about babies. Babies can cry that loud, your baby wanted me to know. He or she was like, Listen to *this*!

"I'm sorry," the real you said, "but I think I'll need to cut our meeting short today."

I said no problem. Gathered my stuff together as you stood from your desk, walked over to the Pack 'n Play, and scooped your baby up. You made what I guess were appropriate soothing noises, patted your baby on his/her distressed back. The baby calmed down a little but not really.

"Let's plan on meeting again next week," you said.

I said sure thing.

You said, "And maybe we should make a deal that you'll send me the first few pages of your paper in the meantime." Which is what you said the last time we met, and the time before that. "Does that sound okay?"

I said it sounded okay.

"And if those first few pages aren't happening, don't beat yourself up," you said. Which, I hate to point out, is the same exact thing you said the last time we met.

I said I would just try to get words onto the page.

"And if words on the page don't happen, you can always try what we talked about," you said. The baby was grabbing at your shirt, which, I now noticed, had a dark spot near the collar from where the baby had drooled.

"The recording?" I said.

You said I'd be surprised how helpful it might be, once I got over the self-conscious feeling of talking into a recording device. Which, again, was the same thing you said last time, including "recording device," which seemed like a needlessly formal way to say voice memo, but I know these digital times must present occasional confusions for someone your age, even though I feel semihorrible for saying that, sorry.

I left your office. I walked outside. The pedestrian mall was quiet that time of day, classes in session, I guess, or maybe not. Maybe it was just quiet because it was quiet. Anyway, I walked past the bench where you ate the Rice Krispies treat, wanting to feel some kind of nostalgia about the day I watched you sitting there, but I didn't feel anything aside from my usual loathing for my sentimental self. Insert feelings of loathing here. Insert video montage of Amy pausing on pedestrian walkway, bookbag slung across her shoulder, gazing remarkably at unremarkable bench. I stood there for a moment, trying to feel whatever while utterly failing to feel whatever, even though it seems I had begun to cry. She said, passively, in past perfect. *It seems I had begun to cry.* My inner Brit finds me anon.

Anyway: your car.

Note sudden leap in time.

So what I was saying was that I was standing in front of your car in the faculty parking lot. How did I know it was your car? Because it was obvious in so many ways—from the year, make, and model, all tilting heavily toward professorial woman, to the incriminating baby car seat thingy in the back, to the professional conference tote bag on the passenger seat, to the fact that I lied when I said I didn't follow you to the parking lot the day I bought the Rice Krispies treat. I absolutely followed you that day, and—uh-oh—on a few others, about which I can only say, Oops. I wish I hadn't done that. Those. I really am sorry. Does it help to know that it's as embarrassing for me as it is probably concerning for you? No? I can understand that. Those scales don't quite even out, do they?

But good news: no one leaves their car door unlocked. Including you.

I made a sudden show of pretending to search for my keys—now where did those pesky keys go?—and then I decided to stop doing that. No one was looking. Still, I imagined you watching me, wondering what I was going to do next but all the while sort of knowing what I was going to do next even before I knew what I was going to do next. Which felt strange and yet comforting too. I wanted you to leave but also stay. Insert meditation on students' willful conflation of professors and parent figures, with all attendant resentment, longing, and unresolved emotions.

"You don't want to leave a note," I imagined you saying, the moment I crouched down and began searching through my bookbag for paper and pen.

"I know," I imagined saying, except what I really did was decide not to write a note after all. What would I write? And I was just sort of crouching there, my sad bookbag unzipped, full of whatever was inside. For a second I admired the faculty parking lot, which seemed nicer than most of the other campus parking lots. But maybe there's no difference whatsoever.

I don't know where the leaf came from. I really don't. All I remember is zipping my bookbag and standing up again, except this time, when I stood, I had the leaf in my hand. A preponderance of evidence says I must have picked the leaf up off the ground.

The leaf seemed on the large side, I guess I'd have to say probably oak or maple or maybe birch. Are birch leaves large? This one was. With thick veins arching out from the stem. Reddish-brown in color, in true fall leaf fashion. Slightly damp on one side. I turned it between my fingers, then held it to my nose. A smell like wood smoke, or dirt, or maybe the inside of a grocery bag. The ends of the leaf were pointy. The stem was thick at the base.

What did you think when you saw the leaf? Did you stop to remove it from your windshield wiper, or had you already gotten behind the wheel before you noticed it, the stem threaded through the wiper in a way that seemed intentional? Did that sort of register with you, the unlikelihood of the wiper impaling the leaf in the unlikeliest of manners? Or was it just like nothing at all? Just a leaf that needed to be removed before you could pull away, your baby settling into his or her car seat, your obligations to your family taking center stage. That's what I would think about too, I guess. I wouldn't care about a leaf. I'd just remove it from the wiper and toss it to the ground. If I wondered anything at all about it, I'd forget about it by the time I got home. Later, maybe I'd think, What was it that I was thinking about when I pulled out of the parking lot? I'd try to think about it, but I wouldn't be able to remember whatever it was. I'd just move on to the next thing I was thinking.

That's how I am sometimes. I bet you're the same way too.

Acknowledgments

AGNI Online: "Teachers" (published as "Homage to Former Teachers")

Atlas and Alice: "My Money-Making Scheme"

Atticus Review: "The Rooms" and "The Whole World"

Bull: "My Lost Decade"

Chicago Quarterly Review: "First Everything"

DIAGRAM: "Interview"

5x5: "So Much"

Flash Flood: "Better"

Flash Frog: "Tell Me and Tell Me True"

Four Way Review: "These Sisters"

Gone Lawn: "Nicotine"

Harvard Review: "You Seem Like an Interesting Person" and "Just One More Time"

Jellyfish Review: "Honey"

JMWW: "Lights"

Laurel Review: "Custodian" and "The Dumb Stuff"

Milk Candy Review: "Cruise"

Monkeybicycle: "The First State

Moon City Review: "Today You Are Green"

MoonPark Review: "Grandfather"

Necessary Fiction: "Retail"

New Flash Fiction Review: "Uncle"

New Letters: "Warranty" and "How It All Fell Apart"

The New Yorker "Daily Shouts": "What Did You Do
    Today?"

No Contact: "When Everything Was Brown"

The Normal School: "Cake"

Northwest Review: "The Clock Museum"

One Story: "Hey, Me"

Overheard: "Long Distance"

Pembroke Magazine: "Wattage"

Pithead Chapel: "Checking In"

River Styx: "Fair Enough"

The Rupture: "Overheard" (also reprinted in *The Best
    Small Fictions 2020*, Sonder Press)

STORY: "Tardy"

The Sun: "That Night, That Morning"

Tiny Molecules: "Mean Moon"

Vol.1 Brooklyn: "The Blanket"

Wigleaf: "The Wallpaper People"

X-R-A-Y: "Bad Cat"